"They'll have to pound a lot harder than that if they want to get through that door. It's about three feet thick, and solid metal."

As they crept down the corridor, the greenish glow became brighter, filling the enormous vaulted room with phosphorescent light.

Five young men formed a protective cordon before a great swollen blob of vegetable mold which covered almost the entire balcony right up to the vaulted ceiling. It was the source of the throbbing phosphorescent light. Swinging his sword with both arms, Derek hacked their legs out from under them.

But the phosphorescent blob was completely enclosed in a leathery membrane, and neither by jabbing not slashing was he able to pierce it with his sword. Derek could feel its malice pulsing toward him like a living force. . . .

A
VISION OF
BEASTS
(Book Two)
The
Second
Kingdom

A VISION OF BEASTS

Jack Lovejoy

Book Two

The Second Kingdom

TOR

A TOM DOHERTY ASSOCIATES BOOK

This is a work of fiction. All the characters and events portrayed in this book are fictional, and any resemblance to real people or incidents is purely coincidental.

A VISION OF BEASTS: THE SECOND KINGDOM

Copyright © 1984 by Jack Lovejoy

First printing: November 1984

A TOR Book
Published by Tom Doherty Associates,
8-10 West 36 Street,
New York, N.Y. 10018

Cover art by Victoria Poyser

ISBN: 0-812-54502-8
CAN. ED.: 0-812-54503-6

Printed in the United States of America

CONTENTS

CHAPTER 1: WEST OF SALUSTON

Jana's bright violet eyes scanned the horizon. She knew that if the hundreds of refugees from Saluston were to be saved from the approaching menace, she herself would have to do it. She seemed to be but a delicate little girl of seven or eight, but that was only her outward appearance. Jana was at least eighteen years old, and female only by courtesy. The cataclysm which had thrown all nature into a mutation panic had affected her own ancestors in mysterious ways, and sight was by no means the most penetrating of her six senses.

She had certainly not needed the reports of the scouts—

the few who had somehow managed to get back alive—to tell her that the agents of the Brotherhood of Diablo held all the northern passes. As expected, they were now transporting the machines pillaged from the defeated Saluston back to their stronghold, somewhere in the west. She had not actually known about the machines, of course. But her penetrating senses warned her of the presence of living things, sometimes even hundreds of miles away.

There were no dense strata of living rock, no sheathings of soft gray metal, to obstruct her senses out here in the open. They extended much farther than they had in the underground sanctuary of Saluston. But although she was always aware of the presence of alien life forms, she was still unable to identify them until she had actually seen them with her own eyes.

So there was no way that she could have recognized the infernal hordes of bats that first time she perceived them, and once she had seen them it was already too late to escape.

She had fallen asleep one night, wearied after a long day's march around one of the dead zones, when she was suddenly awakened by the approach of something nasty. Whatever they were, she sensed thousands and thousands of them swarming the midnight skies out of the south. She warned Derek at once.

Fortunately he had decided to camp for the night inside a defensible structure, something he called a "football stadium," whatever that meant. The survivors had been harried by predators even more than usual that day, and he had wanted some refuge where all possible entrances could be closed, or at least easily defended. Every single door of the structure turned out to be intact, and they were all of metal. The trouble was that it had no roof, and the thousands and thousands of unknown life forms were approaching out of the sky.

But Derek managed to get everybody safely under what he called the ''grandstand'' before the very stars were blacked out by the terrible swarm of bats. It turned out that there had been no real danger of night attack by predators. Even the most terrible creatures roaming this terrible land of scarred ridges and valleys sought cover after dark: caves, burrows, pre-cataclysmic ruins; anything to escape the dark swarm.

The bats themselves were the size of small dog-things, with tiny razorlike fangs; the competition for food among them was so fierce that they attacked any living creature, no matter how huge or formidable, with a hellish frenzy that left not a shred of edible flesh behind. Jana did not like to think about what might have happened to the band of refugees, had they camped out in the open that night.

Other creatures were not so fortunate. The refugees heard the screams of rage and torment echoing halfway across the ruined city, as thousands of bats plummeted down out of the main swarm. Thousands more fluttered hungrily about the barred windows of the grandstand, probing with their hideous snouts for some weakness, as if they sensed the living flesh and blood inside. Every rasp of metal or crumbling stone chilled the refugees with waves of horror.

At last somebody discovered a heap of moldering flags and pennants, and Derek quickly had them bound into torches. But even flames waving back and forth inside the barred windows hardly discouraged the rabid hunger of the bats. Then all at once, as if at some unheard signal, they vanished in pursuit of the main swarm. None of them returned that night.

Never had the first light of dawn been so welcome. Nor did it take them long to discover the source of the screams of rage and torment they had heard during the night. Derek took her with him as usual—riding his great dog-thing Buck, in case they had to move fast—when he went out to reconnoiter.

The fight must have been terrific. The monstrous bear-thing could not have been less than three times the size of Buck, who himself weighed well over a quarter of a ton. It had tried to take cover inside a ruined structure. All that survived was a big fur sack filled with bones. Several bats had been smashed to death in its savage death struggles; several more, wings broken, flopped hideously around the desiccated carcass.

This was their first close look at the bats. If millions of such horrors swarmed the midnight skies, then travel after dark, even to avoid the torment of the sun, was no longer possible.

Twilight was fast approaching. How strange that the sun had now become their greatest friend; in the first weeks after their flight from Saluston it had certainly been their deadliest enemy.

A few of the refugees had once worked as gleaners, collecting whatever edible roots, nuts, leaves, and berries that could still be found on the picked-over hillsides about

Saluston. But even gleaners had only emerged at dawn and dusk. None of the others had ever seen the sun at all—until they had no other choice. Generations of living beneath the mountain had left them dangerously vulnerable to every ray from the sky, and many had suffered terribly from sunburn.

Jana remembered how her own little nose had peeled and peeled until she was afraid that she might lose it. But she was one of the lucky ones. In time she had turned a rich golden color, where many others only burned a painful red whenever they exposed themselves to the sun; some still had to wear special broad-brimmed hats and carry parasols.

At first Derek had tried to bring them relief by traveling at night, and taking cover from the burning glare of the sun. Now the sunlight protected them from the bat swarms, but they had to leave the land soon. For the last few days they had not traveled at all, searching for a safe route through the mountains.

Jana's acute senses reached far beyond the horizon. An endless series of ridges and valleys wrinkled the earth into great rugged folds as far as she could see toward the setting sun. Her senses told her that there were people in that direction, a vast number of people; they also told her of something even more intriguing. Hardly a day now passed without awareness of a being very much like herself, far, far away, beyond the western horizon. Somehow she must discover a safe route. . . .

But what route still lay open to them? They obviously dared not drift any farther to the south, whence swarmed the nightly bat hordes. And she had already been confused

11

too many times into thinking that a mere absence of life promised a safe passage. But bleached skeletons, some monstrously contorted, always warned them of the boundaries of these dead zones, some of which covered hundreds of square miles. At their centers loomed deserted military or industrial complexes. That was what Derek called them, at least.

His library, which for all Derek knew was the last of its kind left in the world, had been his most grievous loss in fleeing from Saluston. But he had discovered other books along the way, even small libraries; although leading and provisioning hundreds of refugees left him little time to do any reading on his own. Even more time-consuming was defense against the predators that harried every route he chose, many so frightful and deadly that Derek himself could only guess what they were.

The ornidons had been their first great challenge out in the wilderness of the sun, and almost their last. Jana could hardly believe how much had changed in just the few short months since she had climbed the stone stairway out of the Abyss, seated on Derek's shoulder.

They were the last to leave. Those straggling into the sunlight above them seemed already half dead from terror and exhaustion; perhaps able to move at all only because what they were fleeing was even more dreadful than what lay ahead. The ravening hordes of Gunks would not follow them—not even the most brutal coercion could have whipped Gunks into facing the terrors of daylight—but the agents of the Brotherhood of Diablo were no strangers to the light. It was a great relief to Jana when they did nothing more than bellow threats and curses from the foot of the stone stairway. Was it because they were so ominously outnumbered? One of them had already been killed in battle. Or was it only because they were so rigidly disciplined? They had been given a mission, and nothing must be allowed to jeopardize its success—not even their raging lust for vengeance.

Whatever their reasons, Derek did not take any chances, and led the disoriented band of refugees as far from the Abyss as he dared before sunset. If the hordes of Gunks came pouring up out of their reeking burrows after dark, he wanted to put at least a few ornidons in the way of any possible pursuit. The wilderness of the sun was indeed a terrible place, but even more terrible creatures stalked the night.

Although ornidons hunted mostly at night, their keen eyes were always alert for any chance at a meal. A female with two devil chicks spotted the very first refugees to reach the rim of the valley. No conceivable pursuers would ever get past an obstacle such as this. Could they themselves?

"Derek says that those are the fastest creatures ever to run on two legs," Jana had remarked innocently to Stinky.

"That's a m-matter of opinion, I reckon," he said as they watched the colossal bird rise out of the arroyo and shake its reeking plumage. "Maybe it's n-n-never been tested."

Jana looked doubtfully up at him and shook her head. "Not even Derek can outrun an ornidon."

"That ain't nothing to m-me, little girl."

It was still daylight, and even the few gleaners who had been out in the sun before felt helplessly naked without their frowsty cells and corridors wrapped comfortably around

13

them. The women and children who had lost their men, fighting off the hordes of Gunks, were close to panic. They shrank together, whimpering and crying out at the sight of the ornidon stalking toward them out of the valley.

Derek had foreseen this danger. He hoped to draw the monster away long enough for the people to cut safely across this corner of the valley; there was a low butte at the far side where they might camp for the night. Tomorrow would have to take care of itself. But how long could even he elude a charging ornidon out in the open? He started down the hill.

"Derek!" Jana called him back.

She had been teasing Stinky all this time, and at last he had accepted the challenge. He nodded resolutely at Derek and trotted down the hillside.

But at first the ornidon just ignored him; the hundreds of refugees cringing together on the hill above were much more tempting. Stinky bounced a stone off its huge beak.

"Yah! Catch m-me if you can, birdie!"

The ornidon glared balefully at him, but then just shook its reeking plumage and continued to stalk toward the hill. Derek didn't know what to do now. They could not go forward; nor could they retreat the way they had come— for all he knew, the agents of the Brotherhood of Diablo were coming up on them even now. And it was almost dusk. The moment the sun went down, whole hordes of Gunks might come pouring up out of the Abyss. The people would not be safe until they were across the valley.

"The chicks!" cried Margo's shrill voice. "Run toward her chicks!"

Then the race was on. Stinky no sooner turned toward the arroyo where the ornidon had left her devil chicks than she screamed and started after him. He threw back his round little head and flew across the scrubby plain like a dust devil. The ornidon thundered after him. For a hundred yards it was not far behind, but it was quickly evident that Stinky had greater speed and far greater endurance.

Meanwhile Eva had taken charge of the refugees, calming their panic and getting them moving. Derek watched with surprise, even with some confusion, but he knew that the ornidon would not leave her devil chicks unprotected very long. He led the way along the path through the foothills, which he knew from his years as a hunter was the shortest route across the valley. Gunnar shambled along at the rear. There were no stragglers.

"Looks like you're really the fastest creature ever to run on two legs," said Jana as Stinky came trotting in just after sunset.

"That's more like it," he said complacently.

They took refuge on a low butte, much like the one where Jana now sat. But few slept that night. The cries and screams of beast-things resounded through the darkness in the valley below, the eternal duet of the hunters and the hunted. Moonrise only made the world seem more terrible, for ghastly shapes could then be seen stalking back and forth through the silvery dimness.

Their second day in the open had hardly begun when the carrion birds appeared, soaring on great wings in and out of the air currents rising above the valley. It was still early morning when Derek came trotting in with a dead boar-thing across his shoulders; but there were over two hundred mouths to feed, and the meat did not go very far.

Eva was more concerned about the sun. The one day in her young life that she had spent in the open had left her too badly sunburned ever to forget the danger. She saw to it that all were protected; she had the gleaners braid hats and cloaks out of dried grass and watched that the warm day did not tempt the children to remove their wraps. Without her care and foresight the sufferings of the people would have been far worse.

Jana was suddenly alert. Shielding her eyes from the slanting rays of the sun, she gazed steadily across the butte. At last she saw a dark form slinking ominously toward her through the scrub of stunted trees and brushwood. Then she heard a menacing growl and turned around.

"Easy, Buck," she whispered. "I think it's only some kind of wild dog-thing. We'll be going back to camp soon."

Buck's hackles rose nonetheless, and she sighed. He trusted her senses, but not her judgment. Derek's huge dog-beast now rose out of the shadows to face whatever was approaching them.

Buck had been a formidable deterrent against the savage packs of dog-things that had harried them through the brush country. He certainly caused the creature now slinking toward them to lose its appetite in a hurry. It scurried away with its tail between its legs.

Buck settled back into the shadows again. Jana still wondered how he could see at all in the daylight; he never seemed to open his eyes. She had spent two whole days making him a special sun visor, but he had only torn it off as a nuisance. It was still a mystery whether he had some way of squinting through his furry eyelashes, or whether he just sensed what was around him. In any case, he was ill-adapted to the wilderness of the sun. Buck would always be a creature of the night.

Which is almost here, thought Jana. The sky was now as rusty red as the abandoned railway tracks that they had followed west for several days, until they were blocked by another dead zone. The string of corroding tank cars had evidently contained something deadly poisonous, for not even the wiry bunch grass lived within miles of the tracks. That detour had been the most discouraging of all.

She heard laughter, oddly distorted by the cavern below the butte, and she scrambled to the edge and peeked over the side. The cavern walls sloped inward, almost meeting at the top; it was a natural grotto, whose crystalline waters glowed like amber in the twilight.

Derek and Eva stood naked at the edge of the pool; both were now bronzed from the sun. They dried themselves and began putting on their clothes.

Jana sat back and tilted her little head to one side. She just had to discover a safe route into the west. Dead zones seemed to be everywhere; detours only led to more detours, and for the last few weeks they had been going around in circles. The predators were becoming bolder and more numerous. Their last trek had been followed every step of the way by hundreds of carrion birds, wheeling above them in lazy, watchful circles. Nor was their present refuge very encouraging.

The cliff dwellings had been the home of some people

17

who had perished a thousand years before the cataclysm. From the miserable country around them, she could understand why. The Saluston survivors could not stay here much longer; their food was already rationed, and the game so elusive and scarce that even Derek sometimes came back empty-handed. But how were they to find their way to the west? She concentrated and concentrated.

She had long known that the plains east of Saluston were lifeless deserts; and although life teemed to the south, it was weird and bestial. Nothing human lived there. The agents of the Brotherhood of Diablo were probably still hovering about the northern routes. They must have fulfilled their mission at Saluston by now, and would surely be looking for a chance to hunt down those who had escaped them.

The west was as intriguing and populous as ever. But how to get there? Were the patches of emptiness that she sensed barren mountains or dead zones? It would have been much easier if the lands around the abandoned railroad were not so deadly poisonous. Surely the rusty tracks led somewhere.

Derek had discovered an old map, stained, brittle, and barely legible. But so many of the old landmarks had been obliterated by the cataclysm that nobody could figure out exactly where they were, not even Margo. "Insufficient data," was her verdict. Derek thought that they were in the southwestern quarter of a land called Colorado.

One other thing still puzzled her. Scouts had reported a shallow, muddy river flowing through deep gorges and canyons toward the southwest; there seemed to be human life in that same direction, somewhere downstream. But it was like no life she had ever sensed before, as if thousands of people were asleep at the same time and never woke up. That was impossible, of course. Maybe they were just too far away?

She wished that she had more promising news to give Derek for the council meeting tonight. But no matter how hard she concentrated, she just could not seem to find anything else.

She rose and stretched. The sun had at last dipped beneath the horizon, and the wrinkled earth was now a lurid red, fast fading into darkness. Only now did Buck open his saucer eyes; they looked questioningly up at her like a pair of green lanterns.

"Let's go home, Buck." She roughed his shaggy coat. "Although there's probably not much supper waiting for us."

She knew that Derek and Eva were now climbing the old trail out of the canyon, and she went to meet them. Buck was not yet aware of their presence, so he padded calmly along at her side.

There was one more thing that she wanted to settle at the council tonight—once and for all. Unlike Derek, Margo had plenty of time to read; she had aquired some textbooks in botany and biology from inside a vehicle that had not quite rusted through. She had memorized them in a matter of hours, and now could not pass a plant or animal without wanting to investigate its properties. She was always feeding the essences of various plants to the little animals that Stinky ran down for her. The store of medicines that she had thus developed had already saved many people from sickness or death, although Margo herself could never be trusted to administer the dosage. She was more interested in experimenting on her patients than curing them. In fact, whenever she found some new plant or fungus with intriguing properties, the children had to be watched.

She had also developed some annoying theories about the value of human life. Especially about poor little Belena, now that there was hardly enough food to go around.

Jana wished that the problem might be settled as easily as Gunnar's wife had settled him. In the same rusty vehicle where Margo had discovered the textbooks, he had found some magazines with the colored likenesses of naked women. The women were all big on top, like Eva, although not as beautiful. They seemed kind of soft and fat by comparison, and it was hard to tell whether they looked sly or just sleepy. Gunnar had taken all the magazines with him, despite the fact that he had never learned to read. Then they had been short of kindling to start the campfire one night, and Gunnar's wife had generously made the sacrifice. . . .

Buck began to whine excitedly, and a moment later Derek and Eva appeared on the old canyon trail below. Jana picked her way down through the scrub to meet them.

"Anything new?" asked Derek, scratching Buck's ears to settle him down.

"Just that one place I told you about."

"Where everybody is asleep?"

"I really don't know what it is." She shrugged. "And the mountains are in the way, so it's hard to tell what's beyond them. It might be a different kind of people—"

"Ones who are awake?"

Jana laughed. "But really, Derek, I've got something

20

else to say at the council tonight. I don't care how smart Margo thinks she is—"

"Nobody is going to harm Belena," Eva reassured her. "Or anybody else. Such food as we have will be shared equally by all."

"That's not Margo's idea. She wants to feed people or not according to their usefulness." She frowned angrily. "And I think I can guess just who Margo has in mind to make the decisions about how useful people are."

"The council will make any decisions," said Derek. "But we have to decide something tonight, one way or the other."

The rusted sign at the top of the stairway was barely legible: ". . . O LITTERI . . . S. DEPT OF INTE. . . ." Nobody knew what it meant, except that it had certainly not been put there by the original cliff dwellers.

But the overhanging cliff and the windowless adobe dwellings secured them against the hordes of bat-things. Nor could they easily be attacked from below, had there been anybody in the barren region to attack them. Some night creature howled eerily in the distance as they crossed the cave floor.

The meat was tough and stringy, and was beginning to turn; it was the last of their dwindling supply. The hotchpotch of roots, stalks, leaves, and wild herbs gathered under Margo's direction was surprisingly tasty; although suspicious eyes watched to see that she ate some of it first. But even this pinched fare had taken the whole day to gather and cook. The prospects for tomorrow were even bleaker.

They held the council in what had evidently been some

21

kind of ceremonial court long ago; the stylized symbols of birds and animals painted on the walls were still surprisingly vivid. The floor had been beaten flat by generations of dancing feet. But the dancers' shouts and howls of ecstasy had died away many centuries past, and it was a somber and anxious people who huddled in the chilling desert air tonight.

Derek rose to address them. As he gazed upon the hundreds of faces looking up at him expectantly, he recalled his mother's dream of someday leading the people of Saluston back into the sunlight, and he now realized that it had been more of a fantasy than a dream.

The world that his mother knew was now as extinct as the people who built these cliff dwellings. The cataclysm had been a terrible and monstrous thing; nature had responded with creatures equally terrible and monstrous, struggling to survive by any means in the new environments created all about them. They themselves would have to continue to struggle, if they were to survive out in the wilderness of the sun. No matter how remote any chance seemed, if it was the only one offered, they had no choice but to take it. Without little Jana they would have had no chance at all.

"We must continue our way west," he said, and his voice resounded eerily through the great cave. "You all know that. You all know that we have reached the end of our resources, that the land is barren, that the savage creatures which have harried us for weeks now are gathering in greater numbers than ever. But somewhere downstream of the river that flows through the gorges and canyons nearby there may be a safe passage. I need scouts to investigate.''

A score of hands immediately shot into the air, and Derek nodded with satisfaction. These were the same men who not long ago had thought only of slinking back to their own snug little cells, letting others face all challenges and responsibilities. Their struggle to survive had done that much for them.

Even their appearance was different. Newcome blood obviously predominated; but among the bizarre shapes and deformities there was now little sign of the flab and spindliness, the sickly pallor and furtiveness, that had prevailed everywhere in Saluston.

Even more important was the difference in morale. Among those with upraised hands were some who had cringed and whimpered like curs when they first emerged into the sunlight. Derek picked the three staunchest.

''Follow the river downstream until you come to a land where there are many people. It should take you four days, possibly five, to get there.'' He glanced at Jana, and she nodded. ''We'll discuss the details before you leave in the morning. Now I think we should decide how best to deal with our food shortage until the scouts return. Suggestions?''

Margo crouched at the edge of the firelight like a hungry cat-thing ready to pounce. But Eva had apparently spoken to her already, and her suggestions dealt only with the most efficient means of gathering and preparing such meager foodstuffs as the barren land provided. She said not a word about distribution . . . at least, not during the council.

Derek had long since realized that people are most efficient and willing to cooperate when they themselves join in the making of decisions. Some suggestions were impractical, a few downright foolish. But others were very shrewd indeed, and it was these that were adopted.

He then brought up the problems of sanitation and the dangers of allowing the children to play unguarded where prowling beast-things might get at them. But this discussion did not get very far.

Jana tipped him a signal, and he quickly adjourned the council. The bat hordes had begun to move up out of the south.

Margo stood waiting for him. She was nine years old now; gaunt, intense, and slightly near-sighted. The months of exposure to the sun had barely tinged her natural pallor. It was the treatment of Belena that she found the most unintelligent.

Derek said, "I thought Eva had settled that with you. I know that the poor creature is blind and helpless—"

"But not so helpless as to be incapable of taking sustenance that might be more profitably distributed elsewhere. Nor is she capable of abjuring the solicitude irresponsibly lavished upon her. Hers is the most extreme example, but there are others whose utility also falls unwarrantably short of the rations with which they are indulged. Things as they are, rather than as they are imagined, should be our guide. Untimely professions of goodness necessarily lead to grief."

Jana said, "You know, Margo, sometimes you sound like an awful stinker. Derek has always been a good leader."

Margo sniffed. "Machiavelli, that wisest of all philosophers, has observed: 'It is necessary for a leader to learn how not to be good, and to use this knowledge and not use it, according to the necessity of the case.' An intelligent observation indeed!"

"Yes," said Derek, "but only intelligent."

Jana tugged at his sleeve, and they all looked southward across the dark mountains. A black curtain drew slowly toward them across the midnight sky. They turned and hurried for cover.

Chapter 2: Rumors of Eden

It took the scouts over two weeks to get back to the cliff dwellings, and only two of them returned. Derek was preparing to call for more volunteers, even debating whether he should go himself this time. The food shortage was now critical. He had managed to bring down some small game, which did not go very far; and the flesh of his only quarry of any size—a strange ungulate with gnarled horns and two tails—was so rank that it was barely palatable. Margo's hotchpotches had to be gathered at greater distances each day, under greater and greater pressure from marauding predators.

Then Jana warned him, and shortly afterwards the two scouts came ambling dreamily into camp, munching the last of some ruby-red pomegranates that they had brought with them, as careless as if the deadly world around them were a garden. But their report could hardly have been more encouraging. They had indeed discovered a lush garden land, which was so delightful that the third scout had actually refused to come back with them. Jana alone was confused.

"You say that there's lots of people there?"

"Thousands," said one of the scouts, as if recalling some blissful childhood dream. "As far as your eye can see, and the whole valley is like one big beautiful garden. Every kind of fruit you can imagine, just begging to be picked."

"And delicious," said the other scout. "Never tasted such fruit. I can hardly wait to get back. Hobie's still there. Says he's never going to leave."

"And the people who live there—thousands of them, you say?—aren't menacing or warlike?" asked Derek. "They didn't attack, or try to capture you?"

"Not a bit of it! We never strayed far from the river, just into one corner of the valley. Stretches on right through the mountains, by the way."

"Then nobody saw you?"

"Dozens of 'em saw us. Maybe a hundred. But they just looked at us and kind of smiled, and went their own way." He lowered his voice. "Not a stitch on 'em."

"Naked as the day they was born," confirmed the other scout. "And young, didn't see no old people. But maybe they live in another part of the valley. Just stayed in the one corner by the river, like I said."

"How many days were you there?" asked Margo. "Or, perhaps more to the point, how many nights?"

They had gathered on the roof of one of the adobe dwellings. The two men grinned and shuffled, reluctant to speak; their guilty eyes looked down at the darkening valley below, where squads of people gleaned the land for such scanty pickings as it might still yield, while armed guards watched for predators. They could not bring themselves to look at Derek the Hunter. But at last they had to confess:

"Well, you see, these gals . . . like I said, uh, they went around without a stitch on 'em. . . ."

"It was Hobie's idea, really," said the other scout. "After the first night, we said we'd better get on back. But Hobie said we should, uh, well, kind of take a better look around. So we stayed a couple more nights—"

"All right," said Derek. "We'll talk about this later. Right now we only want to know how we can get the people safely to this valley." He added significantly, "We've already lost enough time."

He gingerly opened the brittle map and smoothed it out flat. Its colors had faded, its cracked folds barely held together, and it was dominated by numbered roads and highways that no longer existed. But it did have a multicolored inset depicting Agriculture and Resources. At the top of the map were the words WESTERN OIL COMPANY, and right beneath them: *More than just service*.

Referring back and forth from the highway map to the inset, they at last identified the valley that the scouts had discovered. It showed up as an irregular slash of purple through the brown motley that covered most of the region.

The tiny black letters were barely legible: *Fruit, truck, and mixed farming.* Then the two men traced their route along the canyon river.

"Only a couple of spots you got to watch out for," said one of them. "There's one place where there's a little quicksand, uh, right about here, I think. And the cave must be just. . . . Yeah, has to be. Here's the bend in the river."

The other man nodded. "Something's in that cave. But it was getting dark, so we didn't have time to check. Right, uh, here. That's where we found the old houses. Roofs were in pretty good shape."

"But you didn't concern yourselves with roofs while you were in the valley, did you?" said Margo. "Why was that?"

"I believe that they've . . ." Then Derek realized what she was driving at. "Yes, why didn't you worry about shelter at night?"

"Well, uh, we did. The first night, leastways. But then we saw that none of the people there was worried about the bats. Fact is, they never seemed to worry about nothing.

"Just strolled inland a ways from the river, and lay down wherever they found themselves at night. And not alone, neither," he added slyly.

"It's like a dream world, Derek. I remember my ma telling us stories when we was kids about a place called the Garden of Eden. Must have been a place something like this, I think. When are we going back?"

"Yeah, I kind of want to get back there myself," the other scout said anxiously. "Can't be much after noon, right now. Why don't we get started today?"

But Derek shook his head. "It's later than that. Look at the length of those shadows. Now both of you get some rest. We'll be starting at dawn, and we'll need you to lead the way."

Reluctantly the two men climbed down from the rooftop, and crossed the cliff below. Gunnar rose and started to follow.

"Heard them stories about the Garden of Eden when I was a kid," he said. "Fruit hanging from every tree, not a care in the world, and going around without a stitch on 'em." This last seemed to impress him, and there was a glint in his eye. "Kind of look forward to seeing this place myself. I just hope those two weren't telling us a tale. Sounds almost too good to be true."

"I don't think it is," Jana said thoughtfully.

Gunnar lowered. "If I find out those two chuckleheads have been lying—"

"No, I don't mean that they were lying," said Jana. "What they told us is probably what they saw. I just have the feeling that they didn't see everything."

"Well, I intend to see everything." Gunnar chuckled as he shambled across the rooftop toward the stairs. "Better start getting things together, so we can leave as early as possible tomorrow morning." He disappeared, muttering to himself: "Not a stitch on 'em. Well, well, never heard of such a thing."

"Where's Eva?" asked Derek.

"Tending Belena." Jana glanced defiantly at Margo. "She's very sick."

Margo sighed disgustedly, but did not take up the challenge. "The reports just iterated were patently dictated by enthusiasm and clownish lust. I propose that we scrutinize them more coldly."

"You're never very warm," Jana muttered.

Margo ignored her. "The most blatant incongruity is the very existence of these people."

"What do you mean?" asked Derek.

"I should think that it would be obvious to the most casual observer. No people dwelling in such euphoric insouciance could by themselves long survive the pernicious hazards by which they are encompassed. Ergo, something is protecting them."

"The Brotherhood of Diablo?"

Derek felt a sickening jolt of despair. He had read often of the vast herds of cattle that men once nurtured and protected for their own food supply. In fact, the reports of the scouts had sounded oddly similar, except that these cattle were human. Was this valley leading into the west really just some hideous plantation of the Brotherhood of Diablo? Who else was powerful enough to protect so many people—until they wanted them for their own use?

But Jana shook her head. "I don't think the Brotherhood of Diablo has anything to do with it."

"Then who does?"

She shrugged. "I just don't know what's there. Remember my telling you that it seemed like thousands of people were all asleep at once? Well, it still seems that way. And yet the scouts reported seeing people awake." She shrugged again. "Who do you think is protecting them, Margo?"

"Our data are as yet insufficient for even intelligent supposition. But let us not allow unwarranted conclusions to obfuscate our hypotheses."

"You mean dumb guesses?" said Jana. "I just asked a question."

"But you introduced that question with *who*, a substantive referring to a person or persons."

"Well, if these people really are being protected, a person or persons has got to be doing it."

"Not necessarily," said Margo.

The pathetic little basket dropped slowly to the floor of beaten earth. The room had no other entrance but this single hole in the ceiling; what the cliff dwellers might once have used it for was a mystery. It would now be the tomb of a child who had died of old age. There was no hint in these shriveled remains of the creature who had for the space of a summer blossomed like a goddess, then withered into old age and death before their eyes. Had Belena ever reached her fifth birthday?

Gunnar drew the rope up through the hole and heaved the stone slab back into place. There was a chill in the night air, but the swarms of bats had not yet appeared. Some nights they did not appear at all. As the people straggled back to their quarters they glanced apprehensively up at the midnight sky.

"That will be our biggest problem," said Derek. "Finding secure lodgings each night for over two hundred people is going to slow us down."

"The two scouts?" said Gunnar.

Derek frowned and shook his head. "I don't think that we can depend on them. For some reason they only want to get back to this valley they've discovered as fast as they can—no matter what the risks. I'm going on ahead with

Jana and Buck, and maybe some men we can use as messengers.''

Gunnar gnawed at his beard and wiped his big paw back and forth across his forehead. ''I thought we'd keep Jana back with us. You know, to warn us in case of trouble.''

Eva smiled. ''It looks like there should be two of you, Jana.''

''Maybe there is,'' she said, laughing merrily. ''Somewhere beyond this valley that we're going to, even beyond the mountains to the west.''

Dawn was not far off now, but they were all too excited about tomorrow's adventure even to think of sleep. They climbed to the highest roof of the cliff dwellings. Margo was already there, crouching like a cold silver idol in the moonlight. She had not bothered to attend the funeral, considering all sentimental gestures a waste of time.

''Have you made contact again?'' Eva asked quickly, before Jana could say anything sharp to Margo. The two did not get along very well these days.

''Almost every night since we came here,'' said Jana, turning her back on Margo. ''Even once during the day.''

''You mean this person is closest to us at night?'' asked Derek.

''No, he's still very, very far away. It's just that—well, it's kind of hard to explain—that I can find things easier at night. Inside of Saluston it didn't make much difference. But it does now that we're out in the open.'' She shrugged. ''I really don't know why.''

''And this person is far to the west of us?'' said Eva.

Jana frowned. ''I don't think he's very happy.''

''*He*?'' Gunnar asked slyly, and Jana laughed.

"Well, that's just to keep things nice and neat," she said. "But sometimes I have the feeling that he's in trouble, that people are hurting him. I wish we were closer."

"We will be," said Derek. "Although I want to take a very good look at this valley before we enter it. I'm glad, now, that Hobie stayed there. He should be able to tell us some things."

"And I got a few things I'm going to tell Hobie," Gunnar growled.

Margo continued to ignore them; nor was she very communicative the next day. She marched along with the main body of the refugees just as she usually did, holding a book a few inches in front of her eyes and rapidly turning the pages. It was one of her botany textbooks: F. E. Lloyd's *The Carnivorous Plants*. She read with feline intensity.

Meanwhile Derek and Jana had already discovered safe lodgings for the night. Sixteen small double-occupancy cabins surrounded an open quadrangle where enameled vehicles rotted in the sun. All but two of the roofs were still intact, although nearly all the cabins had been fouled at some unknown period by human or humanoid occupants.

A rusty sign with big wrought-iron filigree letters arched over the driveway: RIVERVIEW MOTEL, *Daily Rates*. The canyon river below meandered sluggishly through a maze of beaches and sandbars.

"I think the water used to be much higher, don't you?" said Jana, shielding her eyes from the afternoon sun. "Does it say anything on the map?"

Derek shook his head. "Not as far as I can see." He traced his finger over the brittle paper. "There's a dam about—let's see—about fifty miles downstream from here. At least, there used to be.''

''What's that?''

''A dam? That's an obstacle built across a river to raise its level, so the water can be used to irrigate food plants and manufacture the power for machines.''

''Like those in Saluston? Then the Brotherhood of Diablo must have dams for power, because they took all the machines.''

''There are other ways of getting power to run machines. Other machines, for instance. That's what the Brotherhood of Diablo took from Saluston, along with the machines from its shops. Machines for building other machines. At least, that's what the scouts we sent north seemed to be describing.''

''I don't think there's a dam anymore,'' Jana decided. ''The water's too low. But what's that way off to the east? Looks like a giant spider web.'' She squinted. ''Are those bones laid out like that?''

''Is it a dead zone?''

She tilted her head to the side for a moment, then nodded. ''There's nothing alive down there. And see how the trees are all withered right up into the hills. Are they bones, though?''

Derek nodded. ''The ground is cracked into narrow fissures in the same pattern as the bones. So whatever poisons are here must be seeping up from underground, probably from an old storage dump for poisonous chemicals or gases.''

''And whenever anything comes too close to the fissures they get poisoned?''

"Very good. Margo herself couldn't have reasoned it out any better," he said. "I really wish that you two would make an effort to get along."

"It's not my fault," said Jana. "She's the one who's the cold-blooded stinker, not me."

Derek laughed. "Well, she didn't say a word before we left this morning. I wonder if she's up to something?"

"When isn't she?" said Jana.

What looked from the distance like a procession of strange flowers slowly materialized into the troupe of refugees in their broad straw hats. Eva immediately set to work getting the cabins cleaned and the evening meal prepared. Gunnar fumed at the two scouts.

"One place where there's a little quicksand!" he growled. "If I had trusted you two chuckleheads we'd all be up to our necks by now. Oh, stop shaking like that!" he said disgustedly. "Nobody's going to hit you."

Margo observed the two men as if they were specimens. "Tremor, dryness of the mouth, morbid pallor. Notice also their unusual sensitivity to light, betrayed by rapid and involuntary nictitation. Here, give me your hand." She checked the man's pulse. "Also palpitation of the heart."

"Are you men sick?" asked Derek.

Margo answered for them. "Not ill, but manifesting the classic symptoms of withdrawal from a narcotic drug."

Derek stared in astonishment. He had read books by Dickens and DeQuincy about drug addicts; but where could these two men have gotten narcotic drugs?

"There are three kingdoms," said Margo, like an an-

37

cient sibyl reading the omens, "Animal, Vegetable, and Mineral. There is no necessity that the first must everywhere prevail. The data are still insufficient, but the interstices constringe through the inductive analyses of particular instances. You should indeed take a very good look at this valley, Derek. Look especially to the trees."

"I have spoken!" muttered Jana. "You know, Margo, I think you'd be happiest with your face painted, going around saying mysterious things that nobody could understand. Of course we'll look to the trees. If we don't starve to death first." She shook her head in exasperation. "I don't know what's for supper, but it probably won't be much."

"I'm afraid so," said Eva, joining them. "I had hoped we might get some fish from the river, but we didn't see any. Apparently the water is too shallow."

"That's because the dam is broken," said Jana, raising her eyebrows at Margo.

CHAPTER 3: A Night at the Yacht Club

Derek spotted a squat piebald creature hunkered over a pool near the bend in the river. Or did he? One instant it was there, and the next it was gone. It had been too far away to determine whether the large blotches of pink and brown were its skin or merely its clothing. He checked the map. The cave that the two scouts had warned him about was just ahead.

Jana stood for several minutes in silent concentration, but then she just shook her head. "I didn't sleep very well last night. That crazy laughter kept waking me up."

"It was a bird-thing of some kind," said Derek. "None of us slept very well. What's wrong?"

"I'm beginning to think that this isn't going to be one of my better days. First of all, I can't tell whether the gang just ahead is human or not—"

"Gang? How many are there?"

"Fifteen or so."

The river braided its way sluggishly through islands and sandbars; it could be forded almost anywhere, so crossing to the other side would be little protection. Derek immediately sent one of his men back to warn the others, although it was unlikely that so few—whatever they were—would even think of attacking so many. And the piebald creature had really not looked very dangerous; it was probably not much bigger than Jana.

"What about the valley itself?" he asked. "Are the people there still asleep?"

"That's another thing I can't figure out, even though we're closer now. It's like they're not exactly asleep, but not really awake either. Like somebody who's just falling asleep, or maybe just waking up in the morning. It's hard to explain." She shrugged. "Maybe I'd be more awake myself if I didn't have crazy birds laughing outside my window all night."

"Here, Buck!" cried Derek. The great shaggy beast bounded to his feet, although not even Margo had been able to figure out yet how he could see where he was going during the day with his eyes closed. "You'd better ride Buck for a while, Jana. Until we're safely past this cave. Just make sure that he doesn't stand and fight if we're attacked."

"I can try," she said, digging her little fingers into his coat. "But he won't always listen to me when there's a chance for a fight."

Derek drew his sword as they approached the bend in the river; the three men still with him carried pikes. The cave itself had evidently been underwater when the dam was still intact; but its mouth had recently been cleared of silt and debris, and tiny paths led down to the river.

"They're not all inside," whispered Jana.

At that moment a piebald creature scurried out from behind some rocks and disappeared into the cave. Derek was close enough now to see that the large brown and pink blotches were its skin. Then two more scurried timidly for safety, and he slipped his sword back into its scabbard. There was no danger here.

He was tempted for a moment just to push on to this mysterious valley; it was only a few miles ahead, and his curiosity beset him now like a swarm of ants. But the sun was already sinking toward the west, and they still had no refuge; although the bat hordes had not appeared at all last night.

"For once I wish that they had," said Jana, as they crossed the sandy beaches piled up around the bend in the river. "Those laughing bird-things wouldn't have found it so funny, and then maybe I could have gotten a good night's sleep. Can I keep riding Buck for a while?"

"Ask him," said Derek, gazing downstream into the afternoon sunlight.

He gave himself only one hour to find safe lodgings. Else they would have to return to last night's refuge while there was still daylight. This was their fourth day of marching, and the hordes of bat-things had not once appeared during the night. All the more reason not to get careless.

Near the top of the sloping canyon wall he noticed a fleet of small boats, moored in foundations of sun-baked mud; above them hung a line of ruined docks and a structure built to look like one of the paddle-wheeled steamboats in the Mark Twain book. An old yacht club of some kind? He knew now how high the water level had once been.

The steamboat structure itself was not very big; but perhaps the boats could also be used for shelter—if something was not already using them.

"Jana?"

But then he discovered that she was fast asleep; her head buried comfortably in Buck's fur. He shook her gently and she sat up, yawned, and blinked sleepily.

"Something's up there, beast-things of some kind." She started to lay her head back down. "But I suppose they'll have to be flushed out." She sighed and slid from Buck's back.

She blinked sleepily as she watched them scramble up the slope of sun-baked mud and silt. A moment later there was a hideous yowl, and a big cat-thing and three half-grown cubs shot out of a decaying hulk. Their rear legs were shorter than their front, their ears strangely flapped, their fur the color of sun-baked mud; and they were very angry at being flushed from their lair, although not angry enough to take on Buck. They disappeared down an erosion gulley.

The entire canyon lay in shadow by the time the others finally caught up with them. Eva's natural capacity for leadership was now recognized by everyone; even Gunnar had had to swallow some of his bluster and content himself with implementing her decisions—which, he had to admit, were usually more keen-sighted than his own.

But there was no doubt about what had to be done here. Gunnar had his crew preparing the hulks and structures for the night within minutes after he first came shambling and puffing up the slope. Discriminate growls and cuffs animated the work. There was not much time.

"Might have been safer to go back where we stayed last night, Derek." He frowned and tugged at his beard. "If them bat-things come this way tonight we could be in trouble. Part of the roof's gone from that building up there, and these old boats are rusted out. Most of 'em, anyway. The ones built from stout timbers naturally have lasted the best."

"We'll be in the valley tomorrow," said Derek. "The bat-things don't go there, for some reason. Maybe we're close enough so that they won't bother us here either."

Gunnar started to say something, but then just shrugged and went off to further animate his crew. There was still a lot of work to be done, and the sky was already blood red.

Eva got the people and the remaining food distributed among the various structures well before nightfall. Several of the old boats had metal bulkheads, although their wooden decks had to be jury-rigged in places to make them secure. The people were tired and hungry, and the crowding made tempers short, but Eva had so scattered potential trouble-makers that there were no actual fights.

She and Derek shared a small cabin in one of the boats; they found a lantern there and at last got it lighted. Their relationship had changed utterly since fleeing from Saluston, although they had always been affectionate. Not only was Eva's voluptuous body now as bronzed as his own, but she had at last consented to let him teach her to read. In fact, reading together with her seemed to be the only reading he ever had time for these days.

She had, in fact, puzzled out a great deal on her own, during the years when he had gone out hunting by himself. It did not take her long to grasp the few basic principles that still confused her. *The Wizard of Oz* was the first book that they had read together; then *The Hobbit*. There were a surprising number of books still to be found in the world, especially in the rusting vehicles abandoned everywhere along the old roadways.

Eva also read alone now, and her choice of books was rather singular; at least, Derek found it so. He himself had never read anything about military science or history, but Eva never read anything else these days, unless they read together.

He had found *The Influence of Sea Power upon History* to be heavy going, but Eva had been fascinated. She was now working her way through a book called *On War*, by somebody named Clausewitz. But she was always interested in expanding her vocabulary, and they sat side by side on the cabin's only cot reading *Pride and Prejudice* by lantern light.

It was just after midnight when they were disturbed by a hurried rap on the door. Jana poked her little head into the cabin.

"Here they come!" she cried.

Fourteen other people shared the cabin-cruiser with them,

and Derek was anxious to prevent any kind of excitement that might jar the boat loose from its foundation. It was a long way to the bottom of the slope, and the hull was already in bad condition.

But the corridor was deserted. All that he could see in the darkness were two green lights glowing at its far end. This was one night when he did not want anybody sneaking out on deck and leaving the hatchway open; with Buck posted at the foot of the ladder, this was unlikely to happen. There was no point in waking the others, so they kept their voices down.

"We should be able to see them pretty soon," whispered Jana, standing on tiptoes. "I wish that this window wasn't so foggy."

"Stand on this," said Derek. "The glass is clearer near the top."

Jana clambered onto the stool, her bright violet eyes intent upon the southern sky. The moon hung low, and dark, mossy clouds crept stealthily out of the west. The canyon walls raised the angle of their horizon, and they could not see the black curtain moving slowly out of the south until it was nearly upon them.

Buck growled and sprang to his feet, but Derek was already there to calm him down. The force of the huge beast cavorting excitedly back and forth could send them all crashing down the slope.

"That's the direction of the valley, isn't it?" said Eva. "Hardly any of them seem to be moving that way."

"Very curious," said Derek. "Very curious indeed."

"You'll see what's there tomorrow morning." She smiled at him. "Probably very early in the morning."

"Ow!" cried Jana, holding her ears. "They make the most terrible sound I know, and the worst part is that you can't really hear it."

They were all bothered now by the piercing high-pitched vibrations that were just beyond the range of hearing; Buck's hackles rose and his razor talons shot nervously in and out of his huge paws. Then the whole swarm passed over with the weird fluttering sound of flame.

Heavy bodies thudded against the deck just above their head, and they could hear the ratlike scratching of tiny claws probing for some weakness. Cabin doors began to open along the corridor, and Eva glided gingerly up and back, restraining everybody from any excess movement. Derek had his hands full with Buck.

Most of the swarm had passed over by now; but every structure was still blanketed with hideous black shapes, scuttling hungrily across every surface in search of some means to enter. Derek could not restrain a nervous glance at the hatchway.

"Oh, no!" cried Jana. "One of the boats broke loose!"

They watched through portholes in horror as the wooden hulk gathered momentum. The bats hovered about it like flies around carrion as it slid faster and faster down the slope toward the river below. The instant that it plowed to a halt against a sandbar the bats were all over it again.

"Who's in that boat?" asked Derek.

Jana tilted her head to one side. "Oh, Derek! It's Gunnar's family and some of the old people."

Eva joined them at the window. "The boat is solid. Gunnar always said that he trusted stout timbers more than metal. Maybe the people inside are still safe."

"The bats don't think so," said Jana. "Listen! They're leaving our boat to go down there."

Derek felt sick. Even at this distance he could see that the stern and part of the starboard side had been staved in by the crash. Then the boat was so covered with bats that he could see no more. He only hoped that Gunnar could not see what was happening.

Nearly an hour passed. Jana suddenly surprised them both.

"So far, so good," she cried. "They're all still alive. Maybe Gunnar was right about stout timbers."

Derek glanced up the slope. Gunnar had insisted on taking charge of the structure built to resemble an old-fashioned steamboat; nearly half the people were there, and a firm hand was needed to keep them in order. Also, the structure was built almost entirely of stout timbers.

All at once the bats rose into the air, as if on signal, and fluttered northward down the canyon to join the main swarm. Before Jana even gave the all-clear, Derek saw a bearlike form lumbering down the slope. He slammed open the hatchway of his own boat and leaped over the side.

Gunnar had tears in his eyes as he hugged his children; and he beamed with pride when he learned that his eldest son Rollo was the hero.

"Thought they had us sure," said old Tom. "We was tossed around like puppies in a blanket, but young Rollo here kept his head. Even before we hit bottom he was pulling and pushing folks up to the bow. Then before them bat-things could get inside, he gets those big wooden doors off their hinges, and then we all helped barricade the pilot's cabin."

"Stout timbers every time!" cried Gunnar proudly. "Good lad!"

For once Jana refrained from teasing Rollo, although he was so obviously pleased with himself that it was hard to resist. He still thought that she was just a little girl who was too big for her breeches, and resented the way that his father and even Derek the Hunter deferred to her. But for once people did not ignore him.

Not even Margo. She stood at the edge of his circle of admirers, watching him intently. They were about the same age, although Rollo already showed signs of growing to be at least as big a man as his father.

Jana noticed, and nudged Derek. "Clickety-clickety," she whispered. "The wheels are always turning. I think she's even trying to work Rollo into her plots and schemes now." She muttered, "Cold-blooded little stinker!"

Derek was indeed up early the next morning, well before dawn, in fact. Jana huddled sleepily on Buck's back to keep warm as they marched through the shadows of the broad canyon. All three men who accompanied them carried pikes. Fire-red beetles the size of a man's fist scuttled along the beach, and butterflies with colorless transparent wings dodged in and out of the dull morning light; but there were fewer and fewer insects of any kind as they approached the valley.

Then Derek saw something monstrous beside a pool. It looked like some kind of spiny turtle-thing nearly the size of Buck. He approached cautiously. The creature was dead; there were bloodstains on the sand all around its colossal shell, which was about all that was left of it.

Evidently it had not taken cover fast enough last night. The bats had not left much behind.

The river still braided its way sluggishly around beaches and sandbars; but the canyon seemed to broaden into the west in the near distance. Jana sat up and yawned.

"There's some people ahead, but I think they're even sleepier than I am."

"Directly ahead?" He peered down the shadowy canyon.

"Well, kind of off to the right, maybe a mile or so. But they seem to be moving toward the river." She was silent for a moment. "There are other people, miles and miles to the west, who may be awake. Or maybe just too far away. In any case, they seem different somehow." She yawned again and stretched. "Laughing birds one night and bats the next. When am I going to get some sleep?"

Derek was prepared for anything when they finally reached the valley. But it seemed every bit as lush and blissful as the scouts had reported. Nor did it take a geologist to reconstruct the landscape.

The mouth of the valley was several miles across; broadening with a gradual acclivity toward the west. The rich soil indicated that it had once been a spur of the artificial lake created when the dam was still intact. At least, rich soil made up the few miles closest to the river, where blossoming shrubs and fruit trees grew in junglelike profusion. The land was probably not as fertile or well-watered farther to the west, but there was no break in the lush foliage as far as the eye could see.

The morning sunlight crept down the valley. Then they became aware of people, hundreds of people, strolling leisurely in the same direction.

"They look like they're awake to me," said Derek.

But Jana only shook her head, as if something still puzzled her.

The people were utterly indifferent to their presence; not even the sight of Buck seemed to arouse them in any way. They were all naked, and as plump and brown as the ripe berries teeming on the bushes through which they strolled; but their long hair was matted and unkempt, nor did they look very clean. A young couple began making love without any thought of privacy. The others ignored them.

Fruits, nuts, and berries were everywhere for the picking, and the people browsed among the shrubs and trees like two-legged cattle. But they also nibbled contentedly at a strange ruby-red pomegranate, like that which the two scouts had brought back with them. The fruit did not seem to grow in this part of the valley.

"Well, I'm for breakfast," said Jana.

Derek nodded. "The fruit must be safe, they're all eating it."

He tried the berries on a nearby shrub, and they were delicious. Jana meanwhile was trying everything in sight, and everything seemed to please her. The three men who had accompanied them were afraid that Derek was going to send them back immediately with a message for the others, but he invited them to have their breakfast first.

Then a soft young girl of about fifteen dreamily approached one of the men; she had two of the ruby-red pomegranates, and she offered him one. Whether it was the fruit or the naked girl that most tempted him, he could hardly refuse such an offer.

Derek tried speaking to the people, but they did not

respond. Couldn't they talk? Or were they too indifferent to their surroundings to care one way or the other? He began to understand what Jana meant about people who seemed to be just falling asleep or just waking up.

But as he wandered through the lush groves with Jana and Buck, he came upon a carcass as savaged as that of the spiny turtle-thing on the beach. A squat lizard-thing? A hairless animal? There was not really enough left of it to determine. The bats evidently did raid at least this part of the valley at night.

"We'd better get the people moving," he said. "Where are the messengers?"

"Over there. Two of them, at least. I think the other one has decided to get some sleep." She yawned. "He may have the right idea."

But the third messenger was not asleep. He sat with the soft young girl beside a small brook; they gazed dreamily off into space as if they saw worlds more splendid than the one around them. It took Derek several minutes to get him to talk at all.

"I never felt so beautiful," he said, his eyes half-closed in euphoria. "The towers and staircases just go on forever. . . . I feel like I'm floating in a sea of warm milk."

Derek left him. The person he most wanted to talk to now was Margo. She had warned them about the trees. . . .

Chapter 4: The Second Kingdom

"The explication should be obvious to the most casual observer," said Margo. "Note the alluvial deterioration as we proceed inland."

"The trees and bushes look just as healthy to me," said Jana.

"And what does that tell you?"

"Nothing. But I suppose you will."

It was early afternoon and wispy veils of cloud drifted across the sun. The networks of filaments that hovered over most of the trees were so fine that they were almost invisible. Birds, insects, even a few bat-things hung in weird translucent cocoons from the upper branches. That they were being digested was plainly visible.

"An orchard land artificially watered and fertilized prior to the cataclysm," announced Margo, with a sweep of her bony little hand. "Subsequently the indigenous flora were faced with the stringent environmental challenge of nitrogen deficiency. Cataclysmic mutation and selection determined the response."

"Whatever that means," muttered Jana, who had finally managed to get a few hours sleep before the main body of refugees straggled in at noon. "Why can't anybody eat those juicy red apples, or whatever they are? They look very tasty."

"They must needs be," said Margo, "to disguise the bitter alkaloids which are their most insidious constituent. Gunnar's diligence, pending our return, may be crucial to our subsequent—"

"He'll watch the girls carefully, if that's what you mean. And his wife was watching him." Jana burst into peals of laughter. "But you didn't mention Eva."

"Her diligence is assumed."

"You think she's smarter than Gunnar, huh?" Jana again burst out laughing.

Margo glanced critically up at Derek. "Suffice it to say, she does not read novels by preference."

Derek had not been paying much attention to what they were saying. He still had not discovered a secure refuge for the night; and although there seemed to be relatively few bat-things in the digestive cocoons hanging from the trees here, those few were enough to worry him. Then they came upon a ghastly sight.

"Oh, the poor little thing!" cried Jana.

The half-digested remains of what had probably been a child of no more than four or five years of age hung in a translucent pod just off the ground. Jana approached with a feeling of both pity and disgust.

"Better stay on the path," Derek started to warn her.

"Ow!" cried Jana, as a sticky filament slapped her across the hand. She tried to pull away, but it stuck to her skin. Then a whole cloud of filaments began to drift down out of the tree.

Tugging and tugging, she finally snapped the filament stuck to her hand; but several more hit her before she could escape. Then a flash of silver metal whirled over her head, and Derek's powerful arm snatched her from the ground.

"The monitory configuration of the path—" Margo began.

"Oh, shut up!" cried Jana, as Derek put her down. "I'm almost eaten alive by a tree, and all you can do is spout long words. I wish I was a little bigger, Margo, so I could beat you up."

But she was really more frightened than angry, and at last Derek calmed her down. They took a wide detour around the tree, evidently the path normally taken by the people of the valley. There was a red welt on Jana's hand, and they stopped beside a stream to bathe it. Derek carefully washed the sticky filaments from his sword.

"As we proceed up the valley the nitrogen deficiency in the soil becomes more severe," said Margo. "Hence the flora to the same degree become more dependent upon extracellular digestion to supplement the environmental infecundity."

"Are you saying that these plants get even meaner and hungrier?" asked Jana.

"Precisely."

"Then why do people come to this part of the valley? I wish now that I hadn't." She had now gotten over her fright; but still seemed impatient with Margo.

They came upon a number of people, some idling dreamily in the sunlight, others asleep beneath a species of shrub whose waxy leaves were several feet across. This plant did not seem at all dangerous.

"Phew!" said Jana. "These people aren't very particular about what they sleep in. You'd think they'd dig pits or something."

"There are manifold ways of responding to an identical environmental challenge," said Margo. "Ah, here are the true masters of the valley."

Jana shuddered. "Now I really wish that I hadn't come here. And everything looked so beautiful at first."

The bones scattered throughout the grove were a sickly greenish color; evidently stained by the digestive juices of the trees. Thick, fleshy leaves of verdant green covered the upper branches of the trees; they were only of medium height, with a shiny waxen bark the same sickly green as the stained bones. Clusters of ruby-red pomegranates hung enticingly from the lower limbs, within easy reach of the ground. The leaves surrounding these clusters were as tall as a man and fringed with countless barbed thorns. Once they closed, there would be no escape.

Scores of soft young men and women wandered dreamily through the grove. They seemed only vaguely aware of their surroundings. It was as if not even the field of greenish bones all around them was any of their concern. Only the ruby-red pomegranates mattered to them. This was evidently the only life that they knew or cared about.

"Watch out!" cried Jana, as a soft young man reached for a pomegranate.

But nothing happened. He nibbled at the ruby-red pulp as he turned and wandered dreamily off down the valley. The sun had now broken through the wispy veils of cloud, and golden pillars slanted toward them out of the western sky. Soon it would be night.

"The operative mechanism—"

"Oh, shut up!"

Margo sniffed and turned away. She was obviously curious to observe the entire procedure of enticement, capture, and digestion, but she prudently kept it to herself. Enough that her analyses were now proven correct.

Derek, on the other hand, was appalled. Here and there throughout the ghastly orchard were lumpish clusters of leaves, like huge ears of maize; and yet the people continued to amble indifferently through the trees like grazing cattle. He regretted now that he had not started exploring the valley earlier in the day. His only consolation was that they would at least be protected from the bat swarms—even if they came tonight.

"Could these pathetic creatures somehow be rescued?" he wondered. "If we kept them away from this grove long enough, wouldn't they recover?"

"A futile endeavor," said Margo. "Their corporeal chemistry is by now so inured to the alkaloids that abstinence must superinduce unendurable torments. And even if you should succeed in weaning them from their nepenthean habituation, they would only return here at the first opportunity.'' Then she noticed two children approaching one of the clusters of fruit. ''Must we leave the vicinity immediately? I should like to observe—''

''There's more fruit over here, Margo,'' said Jana innocently. ''Why don't you go pick some and see what happens?''

Derek got them moving back down the valley before they started squabbling again. It was now almost dusk, and hundreds of people drifted idly past them in the opposite direction, moving like cattle at nightfall toward the safety of their stalls. A few offered them a taste of the ruby-red pomegranates; they declined and hurried on.

Then they met an organized procession of their own people, hauling newly woven baskets of fruits, nuts, and berries away from the river. Eva had not been idle while they were gone.

''We may have trouble in the morning,'' she reported, glancing resignedly toward Gunnar, who was evidently having trouble already.

Several men, including the two scouts who had first discovered the valley, were in a euphoric state, and Gunnar shuffled back and forth, growling and cuffing them in a futile effort to keep them from wandering off by themselves. The valley offered some very intriguing sights, and the men had apparently succumbed while Gunnar was looking the other way.

His wife was not looking the other way, however. She marched along right behind him; glaring at him and holding their youngest child in her arms like a living accusation. Gunnar was very careful not to notice her displeasure.

Besides, he was having enough trouble trying to listen to Derek's account of what they had found at the other end of the valley, and at the same time keeping his men from wandering dreamily off into the bushes.

At last he shook his head. "We'll just have to tie 'em up for the night, that's all there is to it. I told them and I told them. . . ." He threw up his hands in disgust. "And we're still about a dozen men short."

"At least the women behaved themselves," said Jana.

The bat swarm did not appear at all that night. Nor were the people troubled by insects, although they had to camp out in the open, with only the deadly filaments of the trees hovering invisibly between them and the sky. Fluffy banks of clouds drifted idly out of the west, silvered at the edges by a gibbous moon. The only sounds were sporadic cries of love in the distance; but even these were strangely feeble, almost infantile.

Not until morning were cries heard closer by. These were also rather feeble, although for a much different reason.

"Serves you right!" snapped Gunnar, heavy-handedly tugging loose the ropes binding up his men for the night. "Any more of your tricks, and I'll make you even sorrier than you look right now!"

This must have been very sorry indeed, and even when his men were all untied they could hardly have seemed more docile. Sweating and shivering at the same time, they wept and sneezed and yawned uncontrollably. Some were sick to their stomach; others were doubled up with cramps, or just stared off into space with chattering teeth. A few of the more desperate at last began to rummage through the baskets of fruit with eager trembling fingers, but there was not a single ruby-red pomegranate to be found anywhere. Gunnar discouraged any further investigation with judicious growls and backhanders.

Derek had by now organized several search parties, each in charge of an especially trusted captain. The condition of the missing men made it difficult for Jana to give the searchers any help, but although the valley was seven or eight miles across, the inhabitants seemed to gather for the night in only a score or so of favored locations. She had no trouble at all pointing out these.

Even after the last of the search parties filed from camp, she continued to stand with her little head tilted slightly to one side. Her frown slowly deepened. At last she threw up her hands and sighed, utterly perplexed.

"Very peculiar," she muttered. "Very peculiar indeed."

"What did you find?" asked Derek.

"Not quite nothing. Which to me seems very peculiar, Derek."

"I don't understand what you mean—not quite nothing."

She shrugged. "I don't either. We should be close enough, but for miles and miles beyond this valley—and the sooner we leave it, the better—it seems almost like a dead zone. No people, not even any animals. And yet. . . ." She shrugged again.

As the missing men were led meekly into camp, one after the other, Gunnar only grew more and more exasperated. "These moonheads have been at it already, every mother's son of 'em!" he growled. "Here, gimme them ropes again!"

The search parties had also found Hobie, the scout who

had chosen to remain in the valley. Stark naked and smiling dreamily through half-shut eyes, he was too indifferent to his surroundings to offer any resistance as he was now tied into the chain with the others.

"Still missing a couple of men," Gunnar reported at last. "Which is it—keep looking or start moving?"

"We'll have to search on the way," said Derek. "If necessary, we can come back and search again tomorrow. We don't want to spend another night here, and it's going to take us the rest of the day just to get the people up to the head of the valley. Here, Buck!" he cried. "Jana, you'd better ride. There's not much time, so we'll have to move fast."

"Take a couple of messengers," Gunnar suggested. "So we'll know what you find. Meantime, I'm going to do some exploring of my own. One of our search parties found something that might be interesting." He beckoned to a spindly little man whose broad-brimmed hat looked as big as he did; his face was mottled with severe sunburn. "Tell Derek what you saw."

"Looked like caves, big caves. You can't hardly see 'em from here, but they're only a mile or so from the head of the valley, away up above the trees."

"I'm going to send some people to find out what's in 'em," added Gunnar. "Might give us a roof over our heads tonight—just in case the bats come back."

While Derek was picking the messengers and loading packs with food for the day—Buck's pack was larger than the others combined—Gunnar's eyes drifted toward some naked young girls who were now beginning to move down

61

to the river for the day. But he kept a firm grip on the rope chaining the men rounded up by the search parties. There were over twenty of them, but they all seemed docile enough. Those rounded up yesterday looked too sick and shaky to resist anything; those just brought in seemed too euphoric to care what happened to them.

Meanwhile Eva continued to move efficiently about the camp, organizing the day's march. Her grasp of the principles of logistics seemed to develop with each new military book she read.

Derek watched her with mixed feelings of wonder and mortification. How could he ever have been so foolish as to believe that a woman had to be continually sheltered and protected? So selfish as to think that only he was capable of making important decisions? Despite the dangers and hardships of the last months, they had never been happier together.

Jana scrambled onto Buck's back, and they fell into line behind Derek and the three picked messengers. With the rising sun at their backs, they left camp and hurried up the valley.

Chapter 5: The Footprint in the Sand

"Ugh!" cried Jana, and buried her face in Buck's shaggy coat. "I don't think we have to search for the missing men anymore."

It was the very tree where Jana herself had almost been captured. Two large gruesome cocoons that had not been there yesterday now hung from its boughs. Derek sent a messenger back to inform Gunnar, and they then followed the beaten path around the tree and hurried on. There was nothing to be done for those two men.

Could anything be done anymore for the pathetic creatures who dreamily wandered the valley all around them?

Derek felt utterly helpless as he skirted the insidious groves, where thousands of soft young men and women grazed on the ruby-red pomegranates like human cattle. Was Margo right? Could nothing save them from a wasted life and a horrible, useless death? It would take an army of axmen chopping for years to fell these groves—in danger every day of being seduced by the enemy while in the very act of trying to annihilate it. Not even the Brotherhood of Diablo was quite so sinister.

Derek gazed thoughtfully toward the head of the valley, which narrowed into a low saddle, less than a mile across. An unbroken hedge, a good twenty feet high, stretched directly from one wall of the valley to the other; so dense and regular—almost like the wall of a fortress—that it looked unnatural and sinister. He could only see three gaps in the entire giant hedge; even these seemed strangely like gates.

"The plants here get meaner and nastier the farther we move up this valley," said Jana. "Maybe in the next valley they're even worse. Isn't there some way we could go around?"

"I was wondering the same thing myself. Your 'not quite nothing' sounds ominous."

"I don't like it either," said Jana. "But how can we turn back now? That's the direction the bats are coming from, and I know there's lots of other nasty things that way too. You're not really thinking of climbing over that ridge, are you?" she asked, following the direction of his eyes, to the ridge on the right. "It must be thousands of feet high."

"There may be an old road or trail," said Derek. "If nothing else, it's high enough to give us at least a good look into the next valley."

"First we'd better take a good look around up there."

"Humans?"

She was silent for a moment, with her head tilted slightly to one side. "Well, if they're humans," she said at last, "they must be very stupid humans. Anyway, whatever they are, there doesn't seem to be too many of them."

"Flowers, Derek!" cried Jana, as they at last reached the first gap in the hedge. "They're beautiful! Oh, smell them! I could just gather them by the armful and hug them to my nose!"

"No, Jana," said Derek. "Don't get off Buck's back. We're not staying here very long."

The gap was just wide enough to admit three people abreast; beyond it stretched a broad alley, shaded by the most exquisite blossoms they had ever seen, blossoms like huge fleshy red peonies. It seemed like the fabled pathway to the garden of Paradise—or perhaps like bloodstained teeth in a dark maw. The musky sweetness of their perfume was hypnotic.

Derek turned toward Jana, but she anticipated him: "Don't bother to ask. I've checked again, and it's all just the same. Not quite nothing."

They turned aside and started up the rocky ridge. For so huge a creature, Buck was amazingly sure-footed on even the most precarious mountain trail; no goat-thing climbed more daintily, despite the fact that he never seemed to open his eyes. The banded rock wall was a museum of vanished eons: primitive creatures extinct for millions of years, the imprints of bizarre plants and animals that no human being had ever seen alive, seashells hundreds of miles from any sea. The climb was so steep in places that even Derek had trouble finding reliable footholds; then he had to stop and help the two messengers. Soon Buck lost all patience and just bounded up the sheer rock wall, like a squirrel-thing up a tree.

"Whew!" cried Jana, when the others had finally joined her at the top. "I never want to make another climb like that again! If we detour through the mountains, I hope it's not this way."

"There's a road a couple of miles back," said Derek, looking down. They were only a few hundred feet above the valley floor, but it was enough of a perspective to see the land behind the mysterious hedge. "Just an ordinary forest, as far as I can see. A couple of small brooks, a few clearings, even a meadow; none of the pods or filaments that are . . ." He peered closer. "There's something down there, Jana. It looks, well, almost human. Do you see it over there, walking through the clearing? . . . Now it's gone."

"Very peculiar, Derek." She shook her head in bewilderment. "I saw it too, but I still can't find it anywhere. Maybe it was just a trick of light and shadows. Take my word for it, there's nothing even remotely human down there." She was silent for a moment, then shook her head again. "If there's anything at all alive, there's only one of it. But it seems to be all over the entire forest."

He looked curiously at her. "That does sound peculiar.

But what about up here? Any of those very stupid humans close by?''

''Not within a couple of miles or more. Whatever they are, they seem to live farther up in the mountains. In the direction of all those big trees up there. But what in the world are these little red and green and purple trees all around us? The stumps, I mean.'' She tapped one with her knuckles. ''Ow! It's as hard as rock.''

''I think it *is* rock,'' said Derek, examining another stump.

Jana muttered, ''Trees that eat people, and now trees made out of rock! If the leaves fell on you, you'd be sliced to pieces.'' She shielded her eyes from the sun. ''Those trees up there look like they're made out of wood.''

''So were these, originally,'' said Derek. ''I've read about petrified forests like this. They're fossils.''

''What's that?''

Derek thought for a moment. ''Well, as far as I remember, when a plant or animal dies, let's say at the bottom of a shallow sea, and is covered by sand or mud before it can rot away, its entire structure may in time be replaced by minerals.''

''Oh, I know what that is,'' cried Jana. ''Minerals, I mean. It's the Third Kingdom.''

Derek looked even more curiously at her. ''The Third Kingdom?''

''Animal, Vegetable, and Mineral,'' Jana explained. ''The three kingdoms. Don't you remember Margo talking about them, and saying that it was not always the First Kingdom that ruled? But I still don't see how you get trees out of rock. These don't look like they fell over and died,

67

and they're exactly like the stumps of real trees. You can even see the bark."

"What probably happened was that some ancient forest was inundated by the sea, and the lower parts covered with mud. The top parts simply died and rotted, but the stumps and roots, decaying much more slowly, were replaced grain by grain with minerals, until they were almost perfect copies of the original trees."

That was all he could remember about the creation of fossils. Once more he regretted that his reading had been so narrowly confined to the library of a professor of literature, the only complete library to survive in Saluston. There were so many questions that he wanted to ask about the strange new world around them, about the mysterious cataclysm that had made it so unlike anything that he had ever read about in his old books. Perhaps the answers lay somewhere in the west, where Jana had told him many people had survived. Or perhaps all that she had really sensed in that direction were the evil hordes of the Brotherhood of Diablo—who had only one answer for everything.

"Let's get going," he said at last. The messengers had by now recovered from their arduous climb, and he had still not discovered anything that looked like a road or trail through the mountains. He caught a glimpse of Eva leading the people up the valley, several miles away. They would probably reach the hedge by late afternoon, and he wanted to join them there at about the same time. He was glad now that Gunnar was exploring a possible refuge for the night.

"You can see the caves from here," said Jana, as she scrambled onto Buck's back. "Let's hope Gunnar doesn't find anything nasty inside. From the Second Kingdom, I mean. There's nothing in that direction from the First—except a few of our own people.''

But as they picked their way across the ridge, Derek noticed her glance back several times toward the land beyond the mysterious hedge. Something there still troubled her; he had never seen her so confused about anything before.

Beyond the ridge lay only another ridge, even grimmer and more rugged than the first, then still another. The entire land seemed to have been gnawed by giant teeth. Wiry shrubs and bunch-grass were the only checks to savage erosion, with here and there a stunted pine hanging grimly to its post, like a forgotten sentinel from some long vanished army. The sun burned down out of a cloudless, blue-white sky; but the winds funneling between the ridges made the heat at least tolerable.

At last they spied a cutting—an old road or highway, perhaps a railroad. But it was miles away, and there was a small mountain stream at the base of their ridge—the only water they had discovered thus far—so it was a good time to stop and eat. Buck was restless, and Jana was tiring in her efforts to keep him under control.

The two messengers were also tiring fast, and Derek saw that they could not go on much longer without rest, perhaps a long rest. One appeared so wilted that he could barely stand.

''Here's how we'll arrange it, men,'' he said as they shared out the food. ''One of you can come with us to explore that cutting up there, while the other remains here. Then as soon as we find out what it is, he can return with the information, and both of you start back together. Jana and I will continue to explore for a while.'' He noticed that Buck had stopped being restless only long enough to gobble down two big pieces of meat. ''You should reach the hedge before the others get there. Tell Gunnar what we've found, and that we'll probably have to retreat toward the cave he discovered for the night. Maybe we can all come back this way tomorrow,'' he added doubtfully.

Buck bounded excitedly down to the stream even before they had all finished eating, but it turned out to be not just a matter of thirst. He snuffled up and down the bank, alternating whines of eagerness with low menacing growls. It was obvious that he had discovered some kind of spoor.

Jana had stood for several minutes with her little head tilted slightly to one side.

''Nothing nearby,'' she reported at last.

''But something has been nearby,'' said Derek, kneeling beside the stream. ''Something big.''

''Oh, it's like the story you read to us that time, back in Saluston,'' cried Jana. ''The story of Robert What's-his-name.''

''Robinson Crusoe?''

''That's the one. But I don't think the footprint that he found in the sand was this big. Whoever made it must have a very big foot.''

''And a very strong scent,'' added Derek, ''if Buck could pick it up from so far away. Where's Glen?'' he looked around.

''Asleep,'' reported the other messenger, who had joined them beside the stream. He gaped down at the huge footprint, which was nearly twice the length of that made by an ordinary man and disproportionately broad. "Should I go wake him?"

"Jana?"

After a moment: "He should be safe here while we're gone, if that's what you mean. I think one of those stupid humans I told you about must have made this footprint. Although if they're that big and that stupid, I'd rather not meet any of them."

"Where are they now?"

"Same place," she nodded toward the trees farther up the mountain. "Although it's hard to be sure, with all these ridges and deep ravines in the way."

Derek pondered the risk. The refugees from Saluston had improved wonderfully in vigor since emerging from their confinement beneath the mountain, but few were very robust. Certainly neither of his two messengers were, since he had chosen them more for fleetness than strength. At last he shook his head.

"Both of you had better stay right here until we get back. I'll take a quick look at that cutting, and then we'll all go back together. If there's any more exploring to be done, we can do it tomorrow. Keep your eyes open!"

But that was exactly what the messenger did not do. Seating himself comfortably beside his companion, he smiled with amused superiority at his snores of exhaustion. Then he settled himself even more comfortably and soon was fast asleep.

Meanwhile Derek and Jana, scrambling from ridge to ridge, circling ravines and deep eroded gulleys, at last reached the cutting.

"It's a road all right," said Jana. "Maybe it will take us all the way around. . . . No it won't. Look!"

"I see it," said Derek.

The highway itself was in good condition, and the cutting was buttressed with reinforced concrete. But less than a hundred yards ahead it passed into a tunnel—or, at least, what had once been a tunnel. The collapse had taken place long ago; small trees were already growing out of the debris. A mountain goat, or perhaps Buck, might have found some way around the collapsed tunnel, but it was obvious that none of the refugees would ever pass that way.

"What about the other side of the valley?" Jana suggested. "Maybe there's a road through the mountains there."

"Whether there is or not, there's no way we can get the people up a thousand feet of sheer rock. It's either this way or through that very peculiar valley beyond the hedge. Maybe there's another road higher up the slope."

"That's getting awful close to those dummies with the big feet, Derek. Even now we're closer. . . ." She suddenly fell silent, tilting her head to one side as if listening. "They're below us! Three, no, four of them, heading straight for our messengers."

"Down, Buck!" Derek fought to calm the great beast, who was growling and prancing nervously back and forth. "Looks like he's sensed them too. Have our men moved out of their way yet?"

After a moment's silence: "I think they're both asleep."

Derek ran to the edge of the cutting and shouted a warning. His voice echoed and echoed through the ridges of the mountain. He shouted again; then got Buck settled enough for Jana to scramble onto his back.

Running, leaping, plunging down steep slopes, shouting again and again from the top of every ridge, they went down the mountainside like an avalanche. Jana was too busy just holding on to concentrate on anything else. Derek struggled to keep Buck from racing too far ahead, where he might in his excitement attack these unknown creatures with Jana still clinging helplessly to his back. At last he grabbed the shaggy beast by the fur and wrestled him to a stop.

"Down, Buck! Down!"

Jana did not have to be told to scramble off his back. Nor did she have to concentrate even then to know what was happening.

Like a terrified rabbit-thing one of the messengers suddenly bounded toward them. Right behind him lumbered a huge creature, a monstrosity like some nightmare ape, but an ape that stood over seven feet high on trunklike legs, as erect as a man.

"Over here!" cried Derek.

The messenger responded instantly, which probably saved his life. Two more of the apelike monstrosities leaped into what would have been his path had he not just turned aside. Derek kept a firm grip on Buck.

"There's three of them," he cried to Jana. "You said there were four."

"The other's where we left Glen."

"And Glen himself?"

She was silent a moment, then shook her head.

The messenger bounded past them with a strangled cry.

Derek raced after him and grabbed him from behind. The terrified man screamed and struggled until at last Derek shook him back into sensibility.

"I woke up just in time," he groaned. "Heard somebody shouting way off in the distance, and those big hairy things—"

"Tell me later," cried Derek, releasing him. "Just don't run away again."

Derek headed back to where he had left Jana and Buck. He expected to find them preparing to do some running of their own, menaced by three bigfooted ape-things. He found Jana laughing merrily at something.

"Up, Buck!" she cried. "Up! They're scared of you!"

The great beast reared up on his hind legs, baring his fangs and clawing the air with razor-sharp talons. It was an imposing sight. Certainly the ape-things seemed to think so; for they were retreating toward the next ridge, afraid even to turn their backs on this great dog-thing which stood nearly as high as they did. Their own fangs weren't very formidable compared to the terrible teeth and claws bared against them.

"Once more, Buck!" Jana cried. "Up!"

This last display sent the huge lumbering creatures into full retreat, leaving only a musky stench behind them as they disappeared over the ridge. Jana was delighted. Even Buck, although his eyes were still closed against the afternoon sun, seemed amused in his own doggish way. They had forgotten for the moment that only one of the messengers had escaped alive.

"They're moving off to the left somewhere," Jana reported at last. "All four of them." But now she too remembered the other messenger, and buried her face in Buck's shaggy coat. "Do we have to go back that way again, Derek?"

"Wait here," he said. "We'll leave as soon as I get back."

One look told him that they must indeed find another way, that even if he were to discover a road through the mountains, he could not bring hundreds of men, women, and children into this country. The messenger had been butchered like a game animal, and all edible parts carried away.

Derek led Jana and the messenger through a roundabout circuit that brought them at last to a promontory overlooking the land behind the mysterious hedge. If that was the only route left open to them now, he wanted a good look before entering it.

Only now, as he gazed down into the strangely verdant forest, did he realize how extraordinarily regular everything was. Its brooks, clearings, meadows, and plantations of trees seemed like a vast artificial garden; the patterns of its lanes and pools—all perfectly round or perfectly rectangular—were more and more evident. The longer he gazed, the more regular were the patterns that emerged. Suddenly it reminded him of something he had seen long ago, at Saluston. Had he read it in a book? Or perhaps encountered it in one of his explorations through the Community as a boy?

"Don't bother to ask," said Jana, misunderstanding his pensive expression. "I still can't find anything down there— except the not-quite-nothing that seems to be everywhere at once. I can see those things moving through the trees as

75

well as you can; those two over there by the pool look like those bigfoot uglies that Buck just scared off. But if I didn't actually see them, I wouldn't know they were there. And look how slowly they move! As if they were sick or exhausted.'' She squinted and shielded her eyes from the sun. ''I can't see them very well from this far away, and they keep dodging in and out of the trees. What are they all carrying?''

''Water,'' said Derek. ''See those two people over there at the edge of the meadow?''

''Oh, that can't be water,'' cried Jana. ''Just two people could never lift a vat that big . . . wrong again! They're pouring it out on the roots of that fat tree. But I can't find them either. Very peculiar, Derek.'' They were both silent for several minutes. ''What are you thinking about now?''

''Just calculating,'' he said. ''If we start at dawn tomorrow, and nothing delays us, then we might just get everybody to the other side of the forest before nightfall.''

''Buck won't let them delay us,'' said Jana. ''Those bigfoot uglies, I mean. Besides, there doesn't seem to be very many of them down there. Unless there's a lot more hiding somewhere in the trees.'' She glanced slyly up at him. ''But we're in no hurry now, because our people won't reach the hedge for an hour or so, at least.''

''All right,'' he laughed. ''We can go back a couple of miles to the road. That shouldn't be too steep a climb for you.''

''I was really only thinking about Buck,'' she said.

The people had already settled down to supper before Jana and Derek at last joined them at the hedge. Derek caught Eva's eye and shook his head: there was no easy detour through the mountains. Then he went in search of Gunnar.

He found him not far away from one of the gaps in the hedge, raging and growling and stomping up and down. The men with him could hardly contain themselves, although they knew it could be a painful mistake to burst out laughing when Gunnar was angry. They watched an exasperated woman scrubbing some yellow dust from the face of a man who did not at all look tempted to laugh.

"Serves me right for sending in a boy to do a man's job," cried Gunnar, tugging impatiently at his own beard. "All I ask him to do is look around a bit before it gets dark. But can this chucklehead even do that much? No, he has to stop and smell the posies!" He growled and stamped his foot. "Give me that rag, and I'll wipe his face for him!"

Derek finally settled him down enough to get an explanation. Gunnar had picked a "volunteer" to enter the gap in the hedge and report back before dark with what he found. But the man had no sooner started up the alley of fleshy red blossoms than for some reason he stopped to smell one of them—and got a face full of pollen.

"Spit it right in his eye," added Gunnar. "So all he can do then is sneeze and choke and come running back here in tears. No, no, he's not hurt." He glared at the man. "At least, not yet."

"Let's wait until morning before we do any more exploring," Derek suggested. "Now what about the caves you found?"

"We're all right there," said Gunnar. "Nothing in 'em, not so much as even bats."

"Maybe we'll never see any more bats," said Jana. "And I certainly hope I never see any more of those bigfoot uglies again."

It turned out that neither of these hopes was to be fulfilled in the days that followed. For the apelike monstrosities she had seen on the ridge were only small wild cousins of creatures bred and trained to be truly terrible. Nor was her hope about the bat swarms long in being disappointed.

"They won't gnaw through these timbers in a hurry," said Gunnar with satisfaction as a barricade was completed across the mouth of the last cave. "Wish we had time to chop down all the man-eating trees in this whole miserable valley. But for once I won't mind if our work's been wasted."

"It won't be," said Jana, as she joined him and Derek at the rough barricades. It was well after dark and the moon had already risen in the sky. "Here they come!"

"The way this cave's facing," Gunnar complained, "we won't even see 'em until they're right on top of us."

"It's facing the right way," said Derek. "I want to see just how far west they swarm."

"Have to fly pretty high if they want to get past that mountain range yonder," said Gunnar. "That, or through some pass we can't see from here. I wonder what's on the other side?"

"So do I," said Jana. "I know there are lots of people to the west, but it's hard to tell exactly where, with so many big mountains in the way." She was silent a moment. "I think we'd better get out of the way ourselves."

"They won't get in here, small stuff," Gunnar reassured her. "Stout timbers every time."

"Didn't you tell the people in the other caves not even to put their hands through the bars after dark?" she asked him innocently.

"Of course I did. It would be kind of stupid. . . . Ahem! I did tell them that, didn't I?" He withdrew his own big paws inside the bars. "Anyway, don't worry about these timbers."

A few minutes later he was very glad indeed that Jana had reminded him about his hands. It was like the attack at the football stadium all over again, but this time the bars were only of wood. The gnawing of thousands of razor-sharp teeth was terrifying, although the timbers were several inches thick, and there was no real danger of anything gnawing its way through. At last, as if by signal, the bats fluttered away in pursuit of the main swarm.

Derek could now get a clear look at the direction they took. He was relieved to see that they did indeed regard the mountain range as an impassable barrier, veering to the north the moment they reached its foothills. Less reassuring was the way the swarm avoided the land beyond the hedge.

"Very peculiar," said Jana. "Very peculiar indeed."

Chapter 6: The Land Beyond the Hedge

"See, that's what happens when you don't do what you're supposed to," snapped Gunnar the next morning. It was just after dawn, but he already had all the barricades knocked down. "Can't walk fifty feet without stopping to sniff posies! Or were you eating them red pomegranates like these other moonheads? Serve you right, if you were."

But the man slowly shook his head; so slowly, in fact, that he almost seemed to be in a trance, although his eyes were clear and wide open. He sat at the mouth of the cave, his back against the wall. His woman crouched beside him. The skin all over his body was gradually assuming the grainy texture of gooseflesh.

"I ain't sick, Gunnar," he swore. "And I never went near them pomegranates when the others did." His voice was strangely hollow, every word seeming to drop more slowly than the last. "It feels like when you hit your funny bone, except it's all over my whole body."

Margo appeared with her store of medicines, but this was like no disease that she had ever seen or read about in her medical textbooks.

"Tentative diagnosis: hypersensitization reaction," she pronounced at last. "Probable etiology: pollen inhalation. Since the data are too perfunctory—"

"You mean he got sick smelling those red flowers, Margo?" Jana asked impatiently.

"I tell 'em, and I tell 'em," muttered Gunnar. "But they won't listen."

Margo sniffed. "As I was saying, the data are as yet too perfunctory for a more positive diagnosis. Now although it is a reasonable supposition that the hypersensitization reaction under which the invalid seems presently to languish indeed emanates from his imprudent inhalation of a pollinic irritant, verification must be contingent upon the introduction of one or more additional subjects into the presence of the identical suspect contagion. The more subjects thusly introduced, of course, the more positive should be our subsequent diagnosis."

"I'll pick the flowers myself, Margo, if you'll sniff them," Jana said sweetly. "You're always sniffing at things anyway."

Gunnar, who had been staring in complete bewilderment, at last seemed to guess what Margo was talking about.

"We got no time for any more sniffing of posies," he growled. "By anybody. If I see one of you moonheads even thinking about it, I'll fix your nose so you won't be sniffing anything for a while. And you women had better watch your kids, so they don't get a blast of that pollen either. Now let's get moving!"

The sick man insisted on walking, but all his movements were so slow and deliberate that at last Gunnar became impatient, and had him carried; although the man denied vehemently—in a strangely hollow and drawn-out voice—that he had been moving any slower than anybody else. He also protested whenever he was carried out of the direct sunlight. Gooseflesh now covered his entire body.

His woman guarded him closely, suspicious that Margo might want to experiment on him to test the properties of some new medicine she had developed. Nor were these suspicions unfounded.

Only when the entire troop of refugees actually stood gathered before the mysterious hedge could Margo get anybody to listen to her. Their experiences among the deadly groves of the valley made all she now said about carnivorous plants seem doubly important. For once she explained herself in terms that even Gunnar could understand.

"Don't see how we're going to get on the other side," he grumbled. "The thing must be a good twenty feet high, and just about as thick. These three openings couldn't be easier to walk through if they were gates. As long as nobody sniffs any of the posies, I don't see why we don't—"

"Are you sure we could avoid smelling these particular flowers, Gunnar?" said Derek.

"Precisely," added Margo. "All carnivorous plants entice their prey in some attractively subtle manner, and the facility with which any creature may penetrate the hedge at these three locations, and these three only, should in itself alert our suspicions. Recall the insidious enticements in yonder groves."

"The promegranates?" Gunnar frowned and wiped his big paw across his forehead. "You may have something there, kid," he said at last. "But them branches look mighty tough and wiry to me. Could take us half the day to chop our way through."

"Then we'd better get started," said Derek. "We can't go back, and there's no other route west. If we have to spend a night in the land beyond the hedge—something I hope we can avoid—we'll just have to make sure that nobody touches any of the plants. And I mean, *any* of the plants." Then a new thought struck him. "But what about the hedge itself? I know that some plants are poisonous to touch."

"That contingency had already been obviated," Margo said rather smugly.

They now became aware of some children cutting or breaking off parts of the hedge, as if gathering twigs for firewood. None had taken harm. Nobody bothered to ask who had put them up to the task, or why.

The hedge was so unnaturally regular that there was no evident weak point. Gunnar spit on his hands, seized an ax and leveled a tremendous blow at its base. It was indeed tough and wiry, but after a few moments' chopping, the work suddenly became easier. Nor were there any poisonous or even irritating juices to hamper the chopping, for wherever a branch was cut it instantly began to seal itself.

"Won't take me an hour at this rate," Gunnar reported, as he stopped to catch his breath. "Couldn't be easier if the hedge wanted us to chop our way through. Here, you moonheads! Clear the branches away behind me. Remember—I've got my eye on all of you."

Those clearing away directly in his wake did indeed remember. Others considered it mere bluster, and slipped away into the trees behind them. The lure of the ruby-red pomegranates was all the stronger for the knowledge that they might soon be forever out of reach. Hobie had been the first to enter the valley and knew exactly where the most succulent fruit now ripened.

The perfume exuding from the natural gaps in the hedge spread a lure of its own, seeming to grow more irresistible as the morning sun rose slowly into a cloudless blue sky. Margo sidled toward one of the gaps in order to observe the effects of the fleshy red blossoms—should their perfume indeed prove irresistible to someone. The children were the most susceptible.

But Jana quickly brought this to Derek's attention, and he posted guards there. Other than a cold glance at Jana, Margo displayed no emotion whatsoever as she turned and strolled away in search of some other phenomena to observe.

For the next hour Margo's curiosity—and growing suspicions—were completely absorbed by the hedge itself. The extraordinary speed with which every branch chopped through by Gunnar's ax sealed itself again was very curious indeed. More suspicious were the branches cut or broken off the hedge by the children earlier this morning. They had not merely sealed themselves again. Instead, they sprouted back toward their original shapes so quickly that nearly every scar in the hedge was already healed.

"Look at 'em!" cried young Rollo. "Like snake-things!"

He had been trying to help his father chop and clear away, until he was chased off as a nuisance. Now Margo had enlisted him to do some cutting of her own. Every single branch he hacked through with his knife instantly sprouted again.

"They wouldn't do that if I had my father's ax," he decided at last. "He's almost through the hedge already, and I'll bet he hasn't been working an hour yet. It's just like a tunnel." Then he added, "I'd be able to handle his ax, if they'd let me. Don't worry about that."

Gunnar did not let anybody else handle his ax. Once warmed to the task, he continued to level one tremendous blow after another at the dense tangle of branches, some wrist-thick and as gnarled as ancient oak. He chopped through them like so much brushwood; nor did he seem to tire, even as the tunnel grew deeper, the branches thicker. At last he even started to wonder if some of the branches were dead or rotten, they were so easy to cut through.

Jana had a flask of cold water ready for him when he finally emerged from the tunnel, flushed and sweating and coated with splinters and wood chips.

Derek, Buck, and Jana plunged through the newly cut dark tunnel, alert for any danger that might lay on the other side. There was none—at least, as far as Jana could discover. All she found was a dense and strangely silent forest, stretching away from the hedge. She could see several creatures, including what might even be humans, moving in the distance, although sight was the only sense by which she could perceive them. She looked at Derek and shrugged.

He disappeared back into the tunnel and reemerged a few minutes later at the head of a column of men, women, and children. Eva seemed to have had them all ready to march at the first signal, and no time was lost getting the entire troupe of refugees through the hedge, encouraged by Gunnar from the rear. Hobie and the others lured back into the pomegranate groves appeared at the very tail of the column. Not even Gunnar noticed how docile they looked, or how their shirts and pockets bulged.

"There's a large clearing, almost a meadow, about ten miles straight ahead," said Derek. "From the ridge I saw a stream there, and a couple of pools on the way. But we don't want anybody to eat anything they might find here, or to smell any of the flowers, or even to touch the plants if they can help it."

Gunnar nodded significantly. "They've been warned already, but I'll remind 'em again from time to time. Do you think we can make it to this clearing you're talking about before dark?"

"We'll have to," said Derek. "I had hoped to be out of this valley by then, but I don't think we can make it. There's an even bigger hedge at the other end."

Gunner groaned. "Oh, well, if it's as easy to cut through as this one, it shouldn't hold us up too long. Maybe we can get out of here before dark after all—if we can keep things moving."

"I suppose we can try," Derek said doubtfully.

And Gunner did try, with all the ursine means of encouragement at his command; growling, boxing ears, cuffing dawdlers left and right, shuffling angrily up and back, although it was really Eva who took effective command of the troop. Her grasp of logistics was now almost that of a professional soldier. She did all the quiet and efficient organizing herself and left the noise to Gunnar.

There were two dawdlers at the hedge, Margo and Rollo. Rollo seemed astonished.

"Just look at those branches slither in and out of each other, like they were weaving a big basket! Why didn't they do that before, when my father first chopped 'em?"

"That is precisely the question," said Margo, peering down at the very base of the hedge with the intensity of a slightly nearsighted cat-thing. "But its ramifications are not presently of such moment as its roots. Dig down here at the base of this—"

A growl from Gunnar sent them both scampering after the others, although he himself seemed intrigued for a few moments at the speed with which the hedge was knitting back together. The tunnel he had worked so hard to chop through was already almost completely sealed.

"Might have to chop a lot faster when we get to the other side," he muttered, as he lumbered to overtake the tail end of the column before it disappeared into the trees.

At the front of the line, Derek and Jana led the way, with Buck padding silently beside them. He also seemed aware of the creatures moving in the distance, but paid no more attention to them than if they had been just so many saplings trembling in the wind.

"Wait a moment, Derek!" cried Jana, stopping suddenly. "Trouble!" She was silent for some moments, then shrugged helplessly. "This is the most peculiar place I've ever been in. I've been checking on the scouts you sent out, as you asked me to, and I think one of them might be in trouble. But there doesn't seem to be anything around him."

"Here, Buck!" cried Derek, and then they were racing through the trees, Jana clinging to Buck's back and giving directions at the same time.

The scout was indeed in trouble; there were plenty of things around him, all of them hostile.

A naked girl of no more than fifteen or sixteen with strangely glassy eyes stood watching him in the middle of a small clearing; the rock in her hand looked so heavy that it was a wonder that she could even lift it. But she just stood there like a tree stump, while huge raptorial bird-things and savage bats dived down at the scout from the surrounding trees. Several of these lay on the ground, as immobile as the girl herself.

The scout was badly clawed and bitten, and he wrestled with a pair of bat-things and a large vulture of some kind. Then all at once the girl started to attack him as well, raising the heavy rock over her head as if it were a pebble.

Derek sprang between them and tried to deflect the rock—and was himself thrust aside. Only a second, more determined, spring saved the scout from having his brains dashed out; but it took all Derek's strength to tear the rock away from the girl. She turned and raised her hands to claw him—then once more froze like a tree stump, gazing past him with glassy eyes.

Meanwhile Buck had rent to pieces everything attacking the scout. Jana was attempting futilely to coax the man to his feet. Then a bat-thing on the ground suddenly came to life again, only to have Buck bite its head off.

"Derek, behind you!" cried Jana.

The ape-thing was well over seven feet tall, like the creatures that had driven them out of the mountains yesterday, but it moved much more slowly, and in fact stopped dead just as it reached the clearing. Derek leapt straight at it and plunged his sword into its heart.

Nothing happened. The ape-thing continued to stare at him with the dead glassy eyes of a doll, and all that oozed from the wound was a sticky resinous fluid which stopped flowing almost immediately. There was no trace of blood.

"And no smell either," added Jana. "Let's get out of here, Derek. I don't think these creatures . . . Watch out!"

Derek whirled and slashed at the buzzard-thing as it dived at his head. Then he slashed again as a huge bat-thing dived down from the same tree.

Meanwhile Jana had at last coaxed the scout to his feet; he was badly shaken and bleeding from several wounds. But for a moment he could do nothing but stare in horror at something on the ground. Then Jana saw it too.

"The bat-thing!" she cried. "Buck bit its head off, and now it's growing a new head. It's still alive!"

Then the naked girl again attacked Derek with outstretched claws; but he dodged past her to help the wounded scout from the clearing. Jana had already clambered onto Buck's back, and they all fled through the trees. There was no pursuit.

"I came across critters like that all along the line," the scout reported, as they bathed his wounds at a forest pool. "They never bothered me. Then I stepped into that clearing, and all at once they started coming at me from all sides.

Tried to run, but they knocked me down and kept dropping on me from above so's I couldn't get up again."

"What about the other scouts, Jana?" asked Derek.

"I've already checked," she said. "No trouble, as far as I can tell."

Nor did they have any more trouble for the rest of the day. Derek and Jana led the way, with scouts posted on all sides. They detoured around any tree or grove that looked at all suspicious, and stopped only twice during the entire march to rest. This land seemed just as tame now as it had appeared to be from the mountaintop. Nothing delayed them; nothing even bothered them, until they tried to leave.

"Told you we'd get here before dark," said Gunnar, as the second hedge loomed before them in the late afternoon sunlight. There were no gaps here, no alleys of red blossoms to entice the wanderers with their perfume; there was only a towering hedge, stretching from one sheer wall of the valley to the other. "Where's my ax? I'll be through this thing before dark, and we'll camp on the other side."

But the first few strokes told him that this might be a tougher job than he thought. These branches were every bit as tough and wiry as they looked. He called for a whetstone, honed his blade, and attacked the hedge with redoubled vigor. He made progress, and armload after armload of chopped branches was cleared away behind him.

"Watch out, Pa!" cried Rollo, running forward with his own small hatchet. "It's growing together behind you."

"Watch out, yourself!" Gunnar swung his ax even more vigorously than before; but now he was trying to

91

chop his way out of the hedge, not in. "Just look at that, will you! It grows together as fast as you can cut it!"

"Not quite that fast," said Derek. "Let's give it one more try. We'll work together at the front of the tunnel, and station men on either side as we move forward, to trim back any new growth. I'd like to be out of this place before dark."

"It's almost like it doesn't want us to leave," muttered Gunnar, as he again spat on his hands. "But we're going to, like it or not!"

Once they got organized, progress was steady and encouraging. The new growth at the sides and top of the tunnel was trimmed back as fast as it sprouted, whole cords of chopped branches were hauled away, and relays of sharpened axes and hatchets were continually passed to the front. Even young Rollo was allowed to whet his father's ax. They were past the halfway point in the tunnel when the attack came.

Eva had organized the entire column into orderly files, ready to dash through the tunnel the very moment it was open. But people were now running helter-skelter for cover; even the armed guards were falling back in horror and dismay.

Derek, hearing the cries, left Gunnar chopping. He took one look, then raced back into the tunnel. "All of you, get out of here! Fast! Keep your axes, you may need them!"

"An hour's work lost for good!" muttered Gunnar disgustedly, the last to emerge from the tunnel. "We'll never get through tonight, at this rate."

"We may never get through at all," cried Derek. "Look!"

Gunnar's chin could not have dropped any faster if it had been disjointed. "What is all this?" he stammered at last. "Hey, small stuff, I thought you said there were no people here. Those sure look like people to me—and bats and bird-things and. . . . Are those uglies with the big feet the ape-things you told me about, Derek?" He tugged uncertainly at his beard. "None of 'em move very fast, though. Why do they keep stopping like that?"

"Whatever the reason," said Derek, "we can't stop here any longer ourselves. That big clearing is only a couple of miles back. They may not follow us there."

He consulted with Eva for a moment; then they were all moving back through the trees—if in no orderly fashion, at least not in panic. Gunnar trotted heavily along at the rear; brandishing his ax instead of his usual warclub.

"You were right!" he cried. "They're not following us. At least, not now. Maybe the whole gang of 'em—whatever they are—plans to hit us after dark?"

"I don't think so," replied Derek. "In fact, I doubt if anything here will bother us after dark."

His prediction turned out to be correct; although not in the sense he had made it. But this was not fully understood until the following morning.

Derek was diligent in placing their camp at the very center of the meadow, as far as possible from any overhanging tree, and guarding every possible approach. Nor did he hesitate to adopt Eva's suggestions for making the watches, pickets, and relief more efficient and dependable. Then he heard a woman sobbing nearby.

"Her man just died," whispered Jana. "The one who got pollen blasted into his face. It happened just as the sun went down."

Gunnar was already bending over the body when they joined him. Even in the dismal firelight the strange graininess of the dead man's flesh was striking.

"I didn't get too close a look at the uglies that chased us from the hedge," he said. "But they seemed to have a grainy look about 'em too. Just like this poor fellow. If it's a disease, I hope it's not catching."

"It's catching, all right," said Margo, kneeling intently beside the corpse. "Although perhaps not so much in the sense of contagion as that of apprehension. Tomorrow may determine whether we all shall indeed be caught."

"Let's just worry about tonight, kid," said Gunnar. "I saw some bats over there by the hedge, and I don't care how grainy they look. What if the whole swarm hits us out here in the open?"

"They deliberately avoided this valley last night," said Derek.

"In other words, let's all keep our fingers crossed," Gunnar grumbled. "But I think you're probably right. Can't see anything else that could get at us out here in this meadow."

"Except perhaps the meadow itself," Margo added cryptically.

Chapter 7: The King of Kings

Not until the very last watch of the night did they discover that they were surrounded. By the time the outermost pickets even noticed, a hedge had sprung up around them and was already higher than the most agile of them could leap. By dawn the tallest could not even see over the top. The hedge seemed to tremble in the morning light, although the air was deadly calm and oppressive. Sprouting branches continued to entwine like sluggish vipers as it grew ever higher and more dense. Fleshy red pods began to appear all around its inner face.

"Can't blast us with that pollen if we all stay right here

in the center. . . .'' Gunnar stopped pacing up and down before the campfire. ''But what if it grows inward? It could have us in range in a couple of days, and then we'd all end up like that.''

He nodded toward where the dead man lay, covered with a blanket. Then he looked more closely. He wiped his eyes and looked again.

''He's still alive! Look, he's moving!''

''No,'' said Jana, ''he's dead. Or if he's alive, it's only like all the other creatures in this valley. Like a tree or a bush is alive.''

''Then over the hedge with him!'' cried Gunnar. ''Here, you, grab an arm and a leg. I'll take the other side myself.''

The hedge now formed a perfect circle, well over six feet high and still growing, completely surrounding the meadow. Even swinging the awakening corpse in unison, with Gunnar's ursine strength behind the heave, they were just barely able to get it safely over the top.

Eva had already begun to reorganize her pickets. All the available men, and even some of the women and larger children were armed, and posted around the inner face of the hedge. They lopped off each fleshy red pod that appeared.

Derek explained, ''The hedge doesn't have to grow any closer. If it saturated the air with pollen, there's no way we could avoid breathing it in.''

''What next?'' Gunnar sighed wearily. ''Seems like everywhere we go there's something we never saw before trying to get at us. Can't always have been like this.''

''It wasn't,'' said Derek. ''And in a few generations,

when all the unfit new life forms created by the cataclysm have been eliminated, the world will probably be much as it was before. Meanwhile we have to see that we're not among those eliminated.''

"Well, none of us will get eliminated so long as we keep them red posies from growing. Wish the hedge itself would stop growing for a while. We'd better start on it soon, or we'll never chop through it today.'' As he looked around for his ax he noticed Jana sitting with her face in her hands, frowning in concentration. ''What's the problem, small stuff?''

"They're fossils!'' she cried. ''That's what they are: fossils! No wonder I can't find them! Instead of the Third Kingdom replacing the Second, grain by grain, it's the Second Kingdom replacing the First. Just like that petrified forest.''

Gunnar stared down at her in wonder. ''Now what are you talking about? You're beginning to sound like that smartypants kid.''

"I think the pollen must get inside something, then start duplicating every little grain, until it looks just like the original thing. Isn't that how it works, Derek?''

"Yes, that's how trees are fossilized, I believe.'' He gazed thoughtfully toward the hedge and the forest beyond.

But Gunnar was still puzzled. ''You mean all those things that attacked us yesterday—bats, bird-things, bigfoot uglies, people—are just plants?''

"Your supposition seems well-grounded,'' said Margo, joining them with young Rollo trailing along behind her. His hands were scraped and dirty, as if he had been digging. ''Although I would question the tense in which it was expressed. Singular, rather than plural. Plant, not plants."

Derek leaped to his feet. "That's just what you said, Jana. That it was not quite nothing, but seemed to be everywhere at once."

"Still does," she nodded.

"Are you saying that all this around us," Gunnar swept his arm outward, "is just one big plant? The whole valley, miles and miles?" He sat down again, and very slowly began gnawing at his beard. "I think we're in trouble," he muttered.

"Perhaps our immediate condition is not so perilous as you have surmised," Margo said rather smugly. "At least with respect to the penetration of the surrounding vegetation."

"We've been digging, Pa," Rollo blurted out. "Guess what we found!"

"I know what you'll find, if you tell me I should start digging tunnels under the hedge."

"No, no," cried Rollo. "We found roots, all over the place, and only a few inches deep. Roots that lead to parts of the hedge."

"Which parts?" asked Gunnar, beginning to see what he was driving at.

But Rollo could only shrug. "It's a whole big network down there, Pa."

"Although its ramifications are as yet indeterminable, it is a reasonable hypothesis that the network—a strikingly dense network—reticulates ubiquitously throughout the valley. So we need only sever those roots—"

"I got it now, kid." Gunnar lumbered to his feet, and

hefted his ax. "We cut all the roots we can, and wherever the hedge stops growing, that's where we start chopping. Come on, Rollo, and bring that whetstone."

They never did solve the complex root network, but by midmorning the last of the refugees stood safely on the other side of the hedge.

"Let's keep moving," cried Gunnar, sweating in streams as the morning temperature rose. "We're just warming up! Same way with the next hedge, lads!"

But it was not at all the same at the boundary hedge; nor did they get the chance to cut a single root or branch. The attack yesterday evening had been a mere skirmish compared to the onslaught that now dived and lurched and leaped at them from all sides as they approached the hedge. Hundreds of human and non-human creatures attacked in erratic waves, charging savagely for a minute or two, then freezing in place, as if to recharge their energy. But they were inhumanly powerful, and they seemed indestructible.

"Don't even bleed!" cried Gunnar, his ax-head sticky and resinous. "Cut their legs off, it's the only way to stop 'em!"

But even this was ineffectual. The number of attackers was just too great, and any severed limb or wing immediately began regrowing. Derek and Gunnar took the brunt of the attack—for once the latter found himself quicker than his opponents in battle—but they were soon in danger of being encircled.

"Fall back!" Derek shouted at last. "All of you! Back into the trees!"

"At least they can't outrun us," Gunnar muttered, as he chopped the legs out from under a naked young man, who was coming at him with a huge, jagged rock.

Once again there was no pursuit. This time they fell back to a small clearing, at the heart of which stood a pool so perfectly round that it appeared artificial. No one had been killed, and the wounded had suffered only bites and talon scratches.

"What do we do now?" asked Gunnar. "Just sit here until another hedge grows around us? We'll have to go to war if we want to even get close to that hedge. Is there any way we can climb the valley walls?"

Derek shook his head. "I already thought of that. But it's a sheer escarpment on either side, and it would take us days to rig slings or rope ladders."

"No chance of them—what do you call 'em, fossils—giving us that much time to do anything." He shook his head. "Looks like we will just have to go to war, far as I can see."

Derek nodded resignedly. "I'm afraid we're going to suffer a lot of casualties. We're badly outnumbered, maybe even worse than we know, and we can't even kill the enemy—just put them out of commission until they grow new limbs, or new heads, or whatever they need to resume fighting. Eva, how can you win a war against numbers like this?"

"By not fighting against numbers like this," she replied. "Sound strategy is always directed against an enemy's weaknesses, not his strength. If this whole valley is really just one big plant, then it must have a heart or a brain or something that directs it all. That's what we should attack."

"But what about these hundreds of other things?" protested Gunnar. "These fossils?"

"Long ago," said Eva, "many, many centuries, there

100

was a king called Alexander the Great. In one of his battles, the King of Kings had over a million men to his thirty thousand soldiers. But instead of trying to fight against such overwhelming numbers, Alexander threw all his forces straight at the King of Kings himself, the heart and soul of the entire host. He fled, and his vast army just melted away."

"Sounds good to me," said Gunnar. "The problem is we don't know where to find our King of Kings, and there's no time to look."

"The solution is really quite simple," said Margo. "Wherever these fossils, as you call them, show the most disinclination to permit the intrusion of aliens, be sure that you will there find the approach to your so-called King of Kings."

"The scout," cried Jana. "The scout who was attacked. They wouldn't let him pass a certain clearing, but didn't bother any of the other scouts no matter where they went."

"But if we send all our forces straight at this vegetable King of Kings, like Eva says," Gunnar objected, "all these hundreds of things, these fossils, are bound to try and stop us."

"Not if we create an effective enough diversion," said Eva. "That is, keep pressure on the hedge with feints and maneuvers, which should keep all the fossils here until it's too late for them to defend their heart, or mind, or whatever does their thinking."

"I'm not sure it actually thinks," said Derek, as he armed himself and packed food for two days. "It might just reply in the same way whenever confronted with the same problem. Here, Buck! I'll send word the moment we discover this thing."

"We'll be ready to move," Gunnar assured him.

Derek, Jana, Buck and Stinky retraced the path through the forest. The artificial patterns of the trees and shrubbery, the streams and forest pools, were more obvious to them now. Derek was quick to point out any striking landmarks by which Stinky could find his way back alone.

"I won't g-get lost," said Stinky, loping along at a pace that for him was merely a comfortable trot.

After a few miles of steady running Derek and even Buck needed to rest. The pool they stopped beside was perfectly rectangular, as was the small clearing that surrounded it.

"I'm getting sore from so much riding," Jana groaned, as she slid from Buck's back. "That looks like a very nice pool, Stinky. Why don't you take a quick dip? It wouldn't do you any harm, you know."

But he stubbornly shook his head. "Water m-makes you weak, and I need all my strength for r-r-running."

"And the longer you run, the stronger you always get," Jana muttered. "Derek, watch out!"

"I see her," he said, drawing his sword.

The young girl had red hair that fell almost to her knees; she entered the clearing with a large metal bucket, which she mechanically dipped into the pool, oblivious of any other presence. She stood frozen, with glassy, staring eyes, while the bucket gurgled full; then she hoisted it like a teacup, and bore it slowly back into the trees.

"I don't ever want to get in her way," said Jana. "Even Gunnar would have strained to lift that bucket. Is this all the food we get?"

"For now," said Derek, tossing Buck a gobbet of meat.

"We don't know how long it's going to take us to reach this thing. Find anything yet?"

She nodded uncertainly. "Maybe it's just a little bit stronger off to the south, in the direction of that clearing where the scout was attacked. But only a little. It's lucky everything is laid out so nice and neat. Stinky should have no trouble finding his way back."

"Don't worry about m-me, little girl. Ain't seen nothing yet that c-can outrun me." He glanced complacently at Buck and Derek.

The latter did not notice; he sat rapt in thought, trying to remember something important, something that he had not thought of in many years. At last he shook his head and rose.

"All this reminds me of something long ago. . . ." He shrugged. "Let's get going. We shouldn't have any trouble so long as we follow the same trail. But things may get dangerous once we turn south—and we'll all have to move as fast as we can."

Broad and narrow beams of morning sunlight slanted directly into their faces as they ran on and on through the forest. There seemed to be fewer human or non-human creatures now, and none tried to oppose them.

"They must all be at the hedge," cried Jana, clinging to Buck's shaggy coat.

"Let's hope Gunnar can keep them there." Derek pointed to a break in the trees directly ahead. "That looks like the way to the clearing."

"That's it, all right," Jana agreed.

There were a few huge bats and bird-things in the trees around the clearing itself, but their clumsy dives were

103

easily evaded. Beyond the trees on the other side were three bigfooted ape-things standing like sentinels before what looked like an open pit.

"They must be guarding something," said Jana. "That's what Margo told us to look for."

"Yes, but what's down in that pit?"

"You folks w-wait right here," Stinky volunteered. "If them ugly galoots yonder—never seen such big feet!—don't h-h-hear me, they won't know I'm there."

"They know we're here already, Stinky," said Jana. "Look!"

"And look behind us," added Derek. "Everything in the forest seems to be moving this way. This must be it."

"But we can't just run and jump into a pit," cried Jana.

Before she could say anything else, Stinky shot past her, and past the three ape-things as well. They all lunged for him at once, like a ponderous trio of sloths trying to stop a cat-thing, but he was already on his way back by then.

"Only h-had time for a peek," he reported. "Ain't n-no pit at all, far as I can see. Looks like a r-ramp with concrete walls."

"Derek, look!" Jana pointed. "They're blocking the way."

The three towering ape-things had now joined hands, forming a solid barrier directly across the mouth of the pit. Meanwhile several other ape-things, as well as humans and other creatures, could be seen converging from all directions.

"No sweat there, little g-girl," said Stinky. "We just h-have to run around 'em and j-jump down. Ain't but a few feet to the r-ramp."

"Lead the way," cried Derek, "before there's enough of them to surround the whole pit. I don't know what we'll do for light, though."

"Might have saw a l-light down here," said Stinky. "Can't be sure b-because I only took—"

"Move!"

Dashing past the cordon of ape-things, they circled the flank of the pit and leaped, hoping Stinky's estimate of depth was reasonably correct. It was. Although the ramp itself was gnawed by harsh weathering, the walls were indeed of concrete, reinforced concrete built to withstand any force on Earth.

"Told you I s-saw a light," cried Stinky, as they plunged down the underground roadway. "Looks like it's going out, though."

"No it's not," cried Derek. "Hurry! It's a door closing."

He was the last to dive through the colossal metal door as it rumbled across the roadway and slid shut with a crash like thunder. The light was a faint greenish glow not much brighter than Buck's eyes but it was enough for Derek to search out some means of securing the door. The guardian ape-things and everything else converging from all over the valley would be lurching down the ramp in pursuit.

Several minutes passed before the door tried to reopen, as if whatever force that moved it needed time to recharge its energy. That was long enough for Derek to find the chain. It had never been meant for securing anything, and certainly the projections on the door and adjacent wall were for other purposes; nevertheless when the door at last made a tremendous lurch to open, the chain held.

"I saw some people moving down there," Jana whispered.

105

"Real people?"

She shook her head. "No, only like the ones in the forest. But how are we going to get out of here, Derek? They're already pounding at the door."

"They'll have to pound a lot harder than that if they want to get through that door. It's about three feet thick, and solid metal." He drew his sword. "Now where are these people you were talking about?"

"Straight down where . . . oh, the light's getting brighter."

"And another door's starting to close. Hurry!"

This time it was a hinged metal door. Once again Derek was the last to dive through. There was no means of securing this door from the inside, and a few minutes later it slowly swung open again. The pounding at the outer door was deafening.

"Probably a battering-ram of some kind," said Derek, as they crept down a corridor lined with glass-doored offices filled with machines.

"There's one of them!" cried Jana. "They're running away from us."

"Or taking up defensive positions," said Derek. "So whatever direction they take is exactly the one we want."

The greenish glow was now much brighter, filling the enormous vaulted room at the end of the corridor with phosphorescent light. This was Buck's natural band of the spectrum, and his great saucer eyes stood wide open.

"It's c-coming from up yonder." Stinky pointed to a balcony entirely encased with glass which overhung a corner of the enormous vaulted room. "Somebody's up there," he whispered.

Row upon row of panels covered with buttons, switches, keys, and tiny glass bulbs faced a towering array of maps and glass projection screens; everything was clean and polished. In one aisle lay baskets filled with vegetable matter, apparently abandoned there by the people who had just retreated up a metal stairway to the balcony above. The greenish glow was still more vivid, and now seemed to throb.

Jana had already slipped off Buck's back, and he padded after Derek toward the stairway, his hackles rising as he sensed his master readying himself for battle.

Five naked young men formed a protective cordon before a great swollen blob of vegetable mold which covered almost the entire balcony right up to the vaulted ceiling. It was the source of the throbbing phosphorescent light. They were only feebly armed with lengths of chain and broomsticks, and Derek, swinging his sword with both arms, hacked their legs out from under them.

But the phosphorescent blob was completely enclosed in a leathery membrane, and neither by jabbing nor slashing was he able to pierce it with his sword. Derek could feel its malice pulsing toward him like a living force.

Then he heard Buck growl, and whirled around. The legless creatures were pulling themselves toward him with their arms. He hacked the arms away and hurled the limbs and torsos from the balcony. He no longer had any doubt that this swollen vegetable mold was the heart or brain of the entire sinister valley. What it was and how it operated were not so important at the moment as how to destroy it. There was only one way that he could think of—a desperate way indeed—and he was down the metal staircase in a few bounds.

"Keep Buck with you till I get back!" he cried, racing from the enormous vaulted room.

Back along the underground roadway he had spotted a line of khaki vehicles. Derek understood enough about such machines to know that their fuel was violently inflammable. He discovered a metal cannister and a rubber hose in one of the offices, and some thick metal bars. He wedged the latter into the hinges of the vaultlike door to keep it open, and raced toward the vehicles. The futile battering at the outer door continued to reverberate like thunder.

The vehicles were hardly rusted at all, although their tires were collapsed and rotted. The first thing he checked was the compartment in front of the passenger's seat, which always seemed to contain an amazing array of odds and ends. Matches! Several books, in fact, with varying numbers and colors of matches inside. Then in the back of the paneled vehicle he saw a tall red can with a capped nozzle. Much better for syphoning fuel. Tossing his own cannister away, he went to pick up the tall red can, and discovered that it was already filled with fuel: a good five gallons.

He went back up the roadway and through the vaultlike door, which strained against the bars wedged in its hinges as it tried to shut. He was still not sure how they would get out of here again—perhaps there were plans or blueprints showing another exit—but they dared not worry about anything else until Eva's King of Kings had been routed. It might be impossible to batter through the outer door, but there was a chance that it might somehow be wedged open.

"Oh, Derek!" cried Jana. "I almost got bit! Those

things with no arms or legs that you threw down from the balcony—one of them wriggled up behind me and tried to bite my foot.''

Two more of them had actually wriggled in front of the metal stairway; their extremities were already beginning to swell with the stumps of new limbs. Derek leaped over them and bounded up the stairs. Five gallons of fuel went a lot further than he had supposed, and the vegetable blob was thoroughly soaked when he tossed the match. He vaulted over the railing just as chunks of scorched vegetable matter began exploding into the air. Jana and Stinky were already scurrying for the door, with Buck right behind them, his tail between his legs. The blob seemed even more violently inflammable than the fuel itself.

Jana stood in the flame-lit office corridor with her fingers in her ears. ''They're pounding at that door like they've all gone crazy!''

''So long as they keep pounding we're safe,'' said Derek, hurrying into the first office.

Improvising torches out of rolled paper, he began searching the desks and file cabinets for anything that looked like a floor plan or blueprint. Most of the cabinets were locked, but he discovered a set of keys, and rummaged every corner of the office with determined thoroughness. Nothing. Only endless stacks of files and rectangular punched cards.

When he reached the fourth office he uncovered a sheaf of printed schematics, but he could find nothing among them that looked like a floor plan showing the route to some possible second exit. The schematics all seemed to relate to various units of some complex electrical device. Yet they all struck him as being somehow familiar, like something that he had once . . . Of course! This was what he had been trying so hard to remember. Years ago, in Saluston, he discovered just such a sheaf of printed schematics behind just such a panel as those in the enormous vaulted room outside: buttons, switches, keys, and rows of tiny glass bulbs. He even remembered the name on the panel, *Selway Computer NC4X.*

From the perspective of the mountain, all the precise lanes of trees and shrubbery, the perfectly round or perfectly rectangular pools, had seemed exactly like one of these schematics. But what was the swollen blob of vegetable mold? What possible source of power had caused its eerie phosphorescent glow? He shook himself. Abstract questions were an unaffordable luxury when every moment of the day was just a struggle to survive.

"At last!" Jana took her fingers out of her ears. "They've stopped that awful pounding."

Derek threw down the sheaf of schematics, and was down the corridor and out into the underground roadway, without looking back. What if they had finally started trying to wedge the door open? But even when he put his ear against its solid metal, he could not hear a whisper of sound.

The underground roadway was beginning to choke with clouds of acrid mist. Jana, Buck, and Stinky followed him to the door, holding aloft the last of Derek's improvised torches. There was no time to search for another exit.

"I've got to open this door," cried Derek. "Be ready to move quick. If they're spread out, maybe we can dodge past them. If not. . . ." He nodded toward where the roadway bent deeper underground.

But the chain had been pulled so taut that he could not budge it, and had to send Stinky back for one of the thick metal bars with which he had wedged open the vaultlike door. He began pounding at the chain, while the others fell back a few steps and braced themselves to run.

The chain snapped, and the colossal metal door slid back a few feet, then stopped. Even through this narrow opening they could see a solid phalanx of enemies on the ramp outside.

Derek sprang out of the opening. "Get back!"

But not a single member of the phalanx stirred; they just stood there, as stationary and immobile as a hall of statues. Even when the acrid smoke began sweeping over them, there was no movement. Derek ran forward, plunged his sword into the chest of a towering ape-thing, and leaped back. Still nothing.

"Follow me!" he cried, and they all wove their way up the crowded ramp toward the sunlight; half expecting to be grabbed by every silent creature they passed.

Blinking at the strong sunlight, rubbing their burning eyes, they stood dazed at the head of the ramp. After all they had been through, it was hard to realize that it was still morning.

"But we haven't much time," said Derek. "The bats didn't swarm in this direction last night—"

"Oh, look, Derek!" Jana pointed up at the trees. "The leaves are wilting."

Chapter 8: The Afflicted

"See those mountains?" Derek pointed due west. "No matter how tired we are, we must keep everybody moving until we're beyond them. Only then will we be safe from the bat swarms."

Jana groaned. "More riding? It's hard to sit down as it is, and Buck is getting sulky and hard to manage." She was silent for several moments, then sighed resignedly. "I suppose we'll have to go on ahead again. All our own people are out of the valley now. Gunnar must have wasted no time chopping through the hedge. They're moving straight toward some other people, just this side of the mountains. And beyond them. . . ." She shrugged. "Maybe when we get closer to the pass up there I'll know more. The higher the mountains, the harder it is to find things."

"Maybe it won't be so hard to find a refuge there after all," he tried to console her. "Some place where we can rest, at least for a while, where every day of our lives isn't a running battle just to survive."

The scene about the forest pool where they rested was like some nightmare autumn. A rain of withered leaves fluttered down out of trees dying before their very eyes, while a burning summer day dominated the sky. The only sound was a coarse slurping from Buck, who dipped his muzzle thirstily in and out of the pool.

"He'll be all right when he's rested a bit," said Derek. "I think that smoke bothered him."

"It didn't do me any good either," muttered Jana, rubbing her eyes. "How long do you think it will take us to catch up with the others?"

"Probably longer than it took Stinky," he said. "But we're going to need him for a messenger again, so I hope he gets a chance to catch his breath before we get there."

"Say, that's a good idea," she cried. "If we walked for a while, it would give him enough time to rest."

"Sorry, but it won't work, Jana. I know it's rough for you, but we have to get the people to safety before the bats start swarming. Here, Buck!"

The hedge was already turning a sickly gray, and not a single new branch had sprouted across the tunnel chopped through to the other side. But it was almost noon, and the mountain pass loomed many miles away; there was no time for congratulations or even for recounting exactly what had happened. They picked up Stinky, and raced on beneath the gleaming sun.

The valley walls rose up on either side, growing steeper and steeper; soon they also began to narrow. There were few trees here, and the track of some cloven-hoofed beast became more and more frequent. They came across a building with a faded blue-and-gold sign bearing the same device as Derek's map: WESTERN OIL COMPANY. But the little one-story structure was much too small to shelter all the refugees from the bat swarms, even for a single night. The scrubby vegetation all around would not shelter them from anything.

Then they came upon the cloven-hoofed beasts themselves; or, at least, flabby leather sacks filled with their bones. There were an unusual number of them. Strange that so many of these creatures had allowed themselves to get caught out in the open at night; for if they had no regular shelter, they would surely have been wiped out long ago. In any case, the bat swarms did not deliberately avoid this end of the valley the way they did the land beyond the hedge. The grisly evidence of their raid two nights ago lay scattered across the landscape.

At last they halted. Jana slid from Buck's back with a groan and danced up and down until she had worked the stiffness out of her limbs. It was past noon, and she was again beginning to cast a shadow. Buck still did not seem to open his eyes; but he was obviously aware of the clove-hoofed spoor all around them.

"Over there," Stinky pointed, "by them thorn t-trees."

Derek shielded his eyes. At least some of the local animals seemed to have found shelter from the bat swarms. The creatures browsing among the thorn trees looked exactly like the one he had brought down before leaving the cliff dwellings: medium-sized, with gnarled horns and two tails. Even Jana recognized it.

"I hope they don't taste as rancid as that other one you caught." Then she suddenly fell silent, her little head to one side, violet eyes intent. "The people I told you about are over in the same direction. There are only about ten of them, and they're all definitely human."

Derek tightened his moccasins and retired the band holding his golden hair out of his eyes. Jana may have determined that these people were human, but the human spectrum had exploded into unpredictable reaches, mentally as well as physically. She had said that the agents of the Brotherhood of Diablo were definitely human.

"They seem to be mostly like us, Derek," she answered his unspoken question.

"And only about ten of them?"

"On this side of the pass. But we're closer to it now, and I think there might be hundreds of people on the other side, maybe thousands."

He thought for a moment. "Then the people ahead might be just a guard-post of some kind. Perhaps to defend the pass itself. Stinky, you come with me. Jana, I think you had better keep Buck out of sight."

She nodded. "He always gets excited and hard to control whenever he does a lot of running."

The strange animals had disappeared; but the mountain spur upon which they had been browsing was less than a mile away, and Stinky tactfully regulated his speed so that Derek could keep up with him. If it was a guard-post, the watch must have been very slack, for they were able to approach completely unseen. Nor were the people at all like guards.

The three young women did not seem deformed in any way. Their loose, long-sleeved gowns covered them from neck to ankles, as if they were ashamed of their bodies. Or perhaps it was only excessive modesty. They were all strikingly plain.

The terraces where they tended rows of vegetables seemed new, built with patient labor up the steep face of the mountain spur. Still newer terraces were even now being constructed farther up the slope; but the boulders behind which Derek crouched screened him all too well, and no matter which way he turned his head he could not see who was working there. Were they armed? From the sounds of their voices he guessed that there were at least three men, perhaps four.

"I'm going to step out into the open," he whispered. "If I'm attacked, run and warn Jana."

Stinky nodded vigorously; he never had to be asked twice when it came to running, especially when there was trouble.

The three women were gathering what looked like turnips of some kind and did not notice Derek at first, nor was he much concerned with them. They were obviously unarmed. But one of the men constructing a new terrace above spotted him at once and cried out. There were indeed four of them; Derek was relieved to see that the weapons they now went scurrying after were only wooden

117

staves. He smiled and raised his arms in a gesture of peace.

"Greetings," he said, although he could not be sure that they spoke the same language. "I come here in peace. Let us talk and be friends."

He saw that all three women now held golden crucifixes toward him. The men also wore golden crucifixes on chains around their necks, but they held staves in their hands and edged down the slope to get between him and the women.

"I come here in peace," he smiled and held out his open hands.

They continued to stare at him in silence. The men were even homelier than the women, although they too seemed free of any obvious deformities. They wore loose shirts and trousers of a grayish homespun cloth; their sandals were only plain leather bindings. But their fascination was more than mere surprise at the appearance of a stranger. At last they lowered their staves and also held their golden crucifixes toward him.

"Gabriel?" said one of them with awe.

"My name is Derek. Let us talk and be friends. Others will soon be arriving, but we mean you no harm."

He was surprised to see them all look up into the sky. Did they really believe that the others would be arriving from heaven? But they did not seem dangerous, and he turned and beckoned. Stinky emerged gingerly into the open, ready to do what he did best at the first suspicious movement by anybody.

They continued to stare at him, as if they could not quite

believe that he was real, or quite trust him yet. The men had lowered their staves, but did not let them go.

"We seek only a roof over our heads, to protect us from the bat-things," Derek assured them, pointing upwards.

Again they looked up into the sky, but now seemed more confused than ever.

"I'm going to send this man back with word to the others," he said. "There is no danger for you. We come in peace."

Stinky backed suspiciously away after receiving his instructions. The moment he disappeared through the rocks, one of the men leaped agilely up the slope. Derek tensed, and his hand gripped the handle of his sword.

But nobody tried to pursue Stinky—a futile project, in any case—or moved to hinder him at all. Then the man cried out in relief:

"East! He goes east!"

They all relaxed, and the women slipped their golden crucifixes back under their gowns and smiled. The men tossed their staves aside and came forward to greet him.

"Welcome," they cried. "Welcome to our humble sanctuary."

"How great are your numbers?" asked one of the men.

"About two hundred," said Derek. "Including women and children."

This seemed to trouble them; not, as he thought at first, because of fear, but only because their sanctuary was humble indeed. They could not shelter anywhere near so many people.

"Loose the cattle for the night," suggested one of the

women. "The demons may not come. Indeed they seldom come this far."

"Two nights ago they came," a man reminded her.

"All the more reason for thinking that they will not come tonight. Nor will the children of Satan afflict us," she added grimly. "Tonight is the full moon."

There were several more terraced gardens; the few people here were evidently quite industrious. The tracks concentrated into a well-beaten cattle trail as they moved up the canyon, and the belling of dog-things echoed weirdly from just ahead. The front of a deep cave had been stoutly enclosed with masonry, so stoutly, in fact, that it was obvious that these people feared more than nightly attacks of bat-things.

The canyon walls narrowed until they were no wider apart than the cattle trail that wound deeper and deeper into the mountains. Several rangy dog-things with busy tails and sharp-pointed muzzles sniffed at Derek's heels as he passed.

"It's not much to offer your pepole," said the man leading the way up the canyon. They had stopped by the stone-fronted cave. "But it is at least secure. Although I doubt that the demons will return here again so soon."

"How often do they come this far up the valley?"

"Two, three times each moon. Seldom more."

The animal smell grew stronger as they proceeded up the narrow canyon. The rock walls rose sheerly on either side, and they were now completely in shadow. Then the canyon suddenly widened into a broad hollow, several hundred feet across. It was roofed over with a lattice-work of boards, branches, and timbers of all sorts and kinds. The acridness of scorched wood filtered through the animal smell, and the lattice-work showed signs of recent repair.

"It is clean, and the best we have to offer," the man said apologetically. "Nor will the Children of Satan afflict you." He added with sorrow and resignation, "Tonight is the full moon."

"The full moon?"

"The Children of Satan torment the . . ." He glanced up at Derek and grimaced, conscious that what he was going to say might sound ridiculous. He was a homely, nondescript little man, nearly a head shorter than Derek, but he carried himself with poise. He finished diffidently, "They torment the most beautiful among them. We escaped and came here three years ago. Four of us have been taken to God, but a child has been born. A beautiful child, with no mark of Satan upon him."

Derek questioned him further. Just beyond the mountain pass to the west, evidently on the borders of an unusually large dead zone, lived a hideous people who worshipped their own hideousness. Beauty was an affliction, to be purged in torment and death, although it seemed that this beauty was really no more than a mere lack of deformity. But these so-called Children of Satan were numerous, and not all the "afflicted" were tormented to death on the night of the full moon.

"The Invincibles come from out of the west," said the man. "They take back with them their tribute of men and women. But they accept only the afflicted, so the Children of Satan find it no hardship."

"And they've tried to recapture you?"

"Several times. But our defenses are too strong, and

they must always return through the pass before nightfall. The last time they came here they discovered our corral and burned it. We saved most of it after they left, but had to send some of our cattle into the night unprotected. The demons fell on them out of the sky.''

"And who are these Invincibles that come out of the west?'' asked Derek, although he already suspected the answer.

"Great, powerful creatures, some even more hideous than the Children of Satan themselves. It is said that they rule all the world from an island called Diablo, in the midst of the New Sea.''

"The Brotherhood of Diablo?''

The man nodded. "Their agents are here already. They will witness the torments of the afflicted tonight, and leave for Diablo tomorrow with their tribute. Unless judgments must be enacted among the Children of Satan.''

"How many of them come here?''

"Three, perhaps four. The slaves that serve their caravans number three score, or thereabouts.''

"Escape would not be difficult, it seems.''

But the man only shook his head. "Escape would only mean recapture by the Children of Satan. The Invincibles discipline their slaves by threatening to drive them away from the caravan.''

"Where will these torments be held?'' asked Derek. "And when?''

"At the Place of Torment, twelve miles through the pass, less than seven straight over the mountain trail. The torments begin when the full moon stands highest in the sky.''

"And you and the others who escaped were sent there three years ago?"

"Nothing has changed since then, for one other has recently escaped from there. He told us things before he died. Thirteen are always selected, a number of great power among the Children of Satan. The thirteen. . . ." He looked quizzically up at Derek. "It is very confusing. For, you see, all of us have known of our affliction since childhood. Our mothers feared for us and kept us hidden from sight. And now you come here, like the picture of Gabriel in the Bible of the old priest."

"Where is he now, this old priest?"

The man shook his head sadly. "He was captured many years ago, while I was still a boy, and sent in chains into the west. The Brotherhood of Diablo has forbidden all holy things." He glanced up at the blue strip of sky high overhead. "We fear that they will learn of our presence here. And now that the Children of Satan have discovered our corral. . . ." He made a gesture of resignation. "We are all in God's hands."

"I remember reading once: 'God helps those who help themselves.' Come with us, my friend. It's obvious that your days here are numbered, and perhaps you can help us evade these so-called Children of Satan. We already have scores of men able to fight."

He nodded thoughtfully, "It may be the only chance we have left. But the land west of here is treacherous, and the Children of Satan know every ridge and valley. None escape their ambushes."

Derek smiled. "They may outfight us, my friend. But, I assure you, they will never take us by surprise."

If Derek's appearance confused these people, the appearance of Eva left them utterly confounded. All their lives they had been cursed and persecuted because of their affliction of beauty, and at last condemned to torment and death. Now it seemed as if all their sufferings had been empty and vain. It was very demoralizing, and they watched her sullenly as if some cruel trick had been played on them.

"If these are the beauties," Gunnar whispered slyly, "I can't imagine what the ones they ran away from must look like."

"We'll know within a few hours," said Derek. "They're holding a ceremony tonight, on the other side of this mountain. No, no," he laughed, "don't look so glum. I'm not asking you to come along."

"I'll go with you if you really need me, even though my arches are about to collapse. It's been uphill all the way." It was only late afternoon, but the hollow was already in deep twilight. Gunnar peered up at the latticework dome and nodded his head thoughtfully. "Looks strong enough to keep the bats out. Let's hope it's strong enough to keep our loonies in—some of them are already getting jumpy. Would you believe that a gang of the chuckleheads actually sneaked back for more of them red pomegranates?"

Derek nodded. "Margo already told me. She thinks that their condition will get worse before the night is over, that they might even become desperate enough to try and return to that valley."

"I'd like to see 'em try it," Gunnar lowered. "You tell 'em and you tell 'em, and then they just go off and do it anyways! I can't keep my eyes on them every minute of the day.''

"Just keep your eyes on them tonight," said Derek. "That's one reason why I'd like you to stay here while I'm gone."

Gunnar nodded sourly. "All right, I will. And they'd better not give me any trouble tomorrow either—no matter how rotten they feel. In fact, we'd all feel better for a little rest. This place looks pretty comfortable. Maybe we can settle down here for a while? My feet would certainly appreciate it."

"We all need a rest, but I'm afraid we can't stay here even another day. Ten people barely scratching out a living for themselves can hardly feed two hundred more. They'll probably be coming with us, by the way."

"Well if we're going to have to fight our way out of here, I suppose we'll need all the men we can get."

"I'm depending more on speed and surprise—and Jana. Evidently these so-called Children of Satan attack mostly by ambush. There are enough people with us to discourage small forces from attacking openly."

"Not bad fighters now," said Gunnar, as they walked back up the gloomy canyon. "At least, when they're not eating things they shouldn't. Can't watch 'em all at the same time, you know. Where's Jana now?"

"Sleeping at the back of the cave with Buck. They're both coming with me, and we may not return before dawn. Eva is ready to mobilize at a moment's notice."

Gunnar gnawed his beard. "So you really think we're going to have to make a run for it? Well, I suppose that's better than having to fight our way out."

"We may have to do both. Even if we slip past these Children of Satan, we're eventually going to have to fight for our place in the sun. Jana says that there are more people to the west than she had suspected."

"And these beauties you're going to spy on tonight work for the Brotherhood of Diablo?"

"They pay them tribute. Which, I suspect, is what all the people to the west of us must do."

"And that's the direction we're going?" He shrugged. "Not that we've ever had any choice."

"No," said Derek. "But I think we're strong enough now to survive attack until we can build a defensible refuge somewhere. I will never pay tribute to the Brotherhood of Diablo."

"But what if they're already waiting for us? You said yourself that their agents come here to collect tribute. Now our men have become pretty good fighters, but from what I saw in Saluston, we'd have no chance against them. Not even you or me." He wiped his big paw across his forehead and shrugged again. "Like I said, we don't seem to have much choice. I can see now why we can't stay here. Wish we had more fighting men, though."

"Maybe we will," said Derek. "That's one of the reasons I'm crossing the mountains tonight. If the agents of the Brotherhood of Diablo are watching a ceremony, they can't also be watching their caravan slaves. With enough warriors we might be able to survive anything but a full-scale assault—which we should be mobile enough to avoid, if Jana warns us in time." He clapped the big, shambling, bearlike man on the back. "Things aren't as bad as they look."

"They look bad enough to me," said Gunnar. "It must have been a lot better for the people who used to live here."

"It was," said Derek. "They didn't know how fortunate they were—until they were unfortunate. Then it was too late." He glanced up at the sky. "It's almost dusk. Time to wake Jana and Buck."

Chapter 9: The Children of Satan

"Somebody's following us." Jana grinned mischievously. "Rollo must have forgotten that his father told him he couldn't come with us."

Derek sighed impatiently. The full moon was rising, and they still had miles to go before they reached the place where the hideous ceremonies were being held tonight. It was only while the agents of the Brotherhood of Diablo were thus occupied that they dared make any move. Nothing must delay them.

"Any danger from the bat-things along this route?" he asked one of the three men from the sanctuary who had accompanied them. "I mean, for somebody returning alone at this time of night?"

"Very little, and only as he nears our sanctuary. Nor are we likely to meet any of the Children of Satan until we approach the Place of Torment. This mountain trail is used mostly by goat-things."

"Nothing in front of us," confirmed Jana. "I've been checking ever since we left. That's why I didn't notice Rollo coming up behind us until just now."

The moonlight turned the mountains around them into towers of black and silver. Black hulks of rock, gnawed into eldritch forms by millions of years of wind and rain, towered out of the plains below like antediluvian monsters rising out of a silver sea. The sky was cloudless, and the cries of strange night-creatures echoed weirdly from every direction at once. The mountain trail was so narrow in places that they could only proceed single file; but at least they were now moving downward.

"He'll have to come with us," Derek decided at last, half angry with the boy for disobeying and half admiring his spirit. "Where is he now?"

After a moment: "Back where those metal cables are strung. . . . No, maybe a little past there. He's moving pretty fast."

"Wait here," Derek said resignedly and disappeared into the shadows.

Jana continued to sit apart with Buck, idly scratching his ears. His eyes were only half open in the brightness of the full moon. Neither paid much attention as the men who had been left behind gathered to confer.

Besides the three men from the sanctuary, Derek had

brought along some of his own men. The former were now completely baffled by Jana; evidently she was not just the dainty little girl that she appeared. But not even Derek's men could tell them why he always consulted her before he did anything. Most believed her to be some kind of mascot.

Rollo himself only believed her to be some kind of nuisance. He had moved cautiously at first, until he realized that the winding trail was too narrow to allow anything to slip past those he was following. If there was any danger, it was not in front of him. The rising moon now lighted his way, and he skipped along like one of the goat-things that normally used this trail.

"Not so fast, youngster," came a voice from above that jolted him like an electric shock. "Didn't your father tell you that it was too dangerous?"

Derek sat on a boulder overlooking the trail; he was almost invisible in the deep shadows. Then he propelled himself into the moonlight and landed right beside the boy.

"I thought. . . . Well, you never know when. . . . Really, only Stinky can outrun me now—and you, of course. And if you were taking Jana with you, I saw no reason, well. . . ."

"Let's get going," said Derek. "We can't afford to lose any more time."

"You mean I can go with? And you're not mad at me?"

"No, I'm not mad at you. Although I don't know how your father will feel about this tomorrow," he added dryly.

Rollo stopped skipping excitedly up and down, and

thereafter followed Derek very quietly—and very thoughtfully. His father had indeed told him that he could not go with Derek tonight. Told him very distinctly, in fact. . . .

The mountain trail wound southwards through a chain of cols, tracks, and defiles; some half buried between walls of rock, some winding precipitously around sheer cliffs. There were many places for ambush, and the men from the sanctuary were increasingly apprehensive about Derek's haste. But he seemed confident that there was nothing lurking in the shadows or around the next bend, although he was seen to glance from time to time at his dainty little mascot, who now rode the huge dog-thing.

They did not halt until they reached the last defile, where the trail debouched onto the plain near a large town. The full moon had not yet reached its zenith.

"You're sure that the caravan slaves are not guarded?" Derek whispered to one of the men from the sanctuary, whose name was Mathew.

"Only by the fear of the Brotherhood of Diablo. None dares molest them, unless they try to escape."

"And the afflicted, as you call them, are kept nearby?"

"The Invincibles choose their tribute first. The thirteen remaining are then sent to the Place of Torment, where the Children of Satan are gathering even now. But there are deadly feuds among them, and all must surrender their weapons before attending the ceremony."

"Then they must have almost finished," said Derek, glancing up at the full moon. It would reach its zenith in less than two hours. "How many people live in the town?"

"None," said Mathew. "It is forbidden. The Children

of Satan only gather here on the night of the full moon. See that large oval structure at the edge of the town? That is the Place of Torment.''

"Where are the caravan slaves kept?''

"Over there, the long roofed structure beside the open space.''

Derek thought for a moment. "Those two over there,'' he indicated the ugliest of his men. "Could they pass in the dark for Children of Satan?''

"Not even in the dark. They are far too beautiful.''

"Are there guards or patrols around the town during the ceremony?''

"Who would attack? The Children of Satan fear only the Invincibles, and so long as they pay them tribute. . . .''

"Will you go down there with me, Mathew? I need somebody who knows the plan of this town, this Place of Torment as you call it.''

The man hesitated; he knew far better than Derek what would happen to them if they were captured. But at last he agreed.

Derek decided against asking for any more volunteers to enter the town with him; a few men would do him no good in a fight, but would increase the chance of detection and encumber any possible escape.

"You stay right here with these others, youngster,'' he said sternly to Rollo. "Understand? I may need you to take a message to your father. Jana, what about the swarm of bat-things?''

She was silent for an unusually long time; then shrugged. "Too far away, Derek. But I'm usually able to find them by this time of night, if they come this way at all.''

He frowned. "It's still too great a risk."

"I'm not afraid of bat-things," cried Rollo. "You saw what I did when our boat crashed."

"And it was well done," Derek said. "But I was thinking of all our people. Marching by night is too great a risk, even if it is only a few miles to the pass." Then he shook his head. "But if we wait until morning, the element of surprise will be lost. If these so-called Children of Satan are all gathered here tonight, it may be our best chance to slip through their territory unseen."

"Some will see you," said Mathew. "But perhaps not enough to attack such numbers as yours. Only the warriors come here to the Place of Torment."

"And surrender their weapons," Derek added thoughtfully. "Where are they kept?"

The man moved his head from side to side, then stood on his tiptoes. "You can't see it from here. It's just behind that concrete structure—"

"With the central tower? Yes, I see it. Is the building where the weapons are kept also of concrete?"

"Brick. But it is well guarded throughout the ceremonies. As I say, there are deadly feuds among the Children of Satan."

"I'm sorry now that I didn't make better plans before I left," said Derek. "But there was no time, and I never expected such an opportunity. Is there some safe rendezvous close to the pass? We could meet the others there as soon after dawn as possible, and follow the northern route out of the country."

"You must follow the northern route. Nothing can live to the south, not even beast-things." He beckoned to one of the other men from the sanctuary. "Reuben, here, is from the northern valleys—"

"Just a moment," said Derek, summoning the small band close. "I want everybody to know where we're going to meet, in case we lose contact with each other."

After Reuben and Mathew settled their rendezvous and the most likely route out of the country, Derek set everybody on the way to his respective assignment. Buck sensed the excitement and had to be calmed down before Jana could clamber onto his back. Then they were moving in a silent file down the hillside. The Children of Satan could now be seen, straggling grotesquely through the silver light as they converged on the town below.

Rollo obediently stayed behind with the two other men from the sanctuary and three of his own people. He was not afraid of bringing a message home to his father, through swarms of bat-things, or anything else. He was more afraid of the message his father might bring home to him when he learned that he had run off tonight. . . .

Derek posted his men in the ruins of a structure north of the town, ready to act as guides or messengers. A few pikemen more or less would do him no good, but he still needed help of another kind.

"You're certain that those two men could not pass as Children of Satan?" he whispered to Mathew. "Even in the dark, for only a few minutes."

"It might be tried," he said doubtfully. "If it is absolutely vital to your plans. But they must not let themselves be seen in the light. Their beauty would immediately arouse suspicion."

The two ugly men agreed to accompany them; but they

refused to leave their pikes behind, although these seemed only a useless encumbrance to Derek.

"Stay close to Buck, Jana," he whispered.

"Don't worry about that. Not if those two are beauties compared to what we're going to meet in town."

A hatch-work of white lines was still visible on the weathered asphalt surface, and a number of rusting vehicles were scattered about. Beside this broad open space stretched the roofed building where the caravan slaves were penned for the night. The huge sign that rose into the night in front of the building could still be read clearly in the bright moonlight: ARCADIA ROLLER RINK. There were lights inside the building, but no sign of guards.

Leaving the others in the shadows, Derek circled the entire structure. There were several doors, all evidently opening outward, but their handles were easily barred with lengths of pipe, boards, cables—whatever he could find. There were no windows.

"The Brotherhood of Diablo is here," Jana whispered, the moment he returned. "We just saw two of them, and a gang of uglies that make even the Gunks look pretty. Were those really their faces, or were they wearing masks?"

"There is a green desert worm," said Mathew, "with which the Children of Satan test their manhood. They place the worms in cuts or sores on their faces—"

"Ugh!" cried Jana, and buried her face in Buck's shaggy coat.

"And they were hideous to begin with?" said Derek.

Mathew nodded. "That is why I said your men must not be seen in the light."

"They won't be. But where was everybody going?"

"To the Place of Torment." Mathew pointed up at the sky; the full moon was nearing its zenith. "The tribute has now been selected, and the Invincibles go—"

He suddenly fell silent, and they all drew back into the shadows. An abject file of men and women, bound together by a long rope around each of their necks, was being driven toward them.

"The tribute," whispered Mathew.

"What about the others?"

Mathew shook his head sadly. "They have already been taken to the Place of Torment. There is no hope for them."

"And yet you and your friends escaped."

"We were selected as tribute. One of the caravan slaves had a knife, and he helped us cut our bonds. We escaped in the night from this very building, while our guards slept."

"Well, we can't wait for them to fall asleep tonight. How many are there?"

"Five. But they may not remain—at least, not all of them. Only two remained the night we escaped. Mostly to prevent fights among the caravan slaves."

Derek was now glad that his men had brought their pikes after all. A few moments later three creatures so gruesome that they scarcely looked human left the building and hurried off toward the Place of Torment. Derek charged through the entrance the moment they were out of sight, with Mathew and the two pikemen right behind him.

A large foyer with long rows of benches, lockers, and glass counters opened onto an elliptical floor that stretched, without pillars or obstructions, the entire length of the building. On a dais at the far end stood a large musical instrument of some kind; the placard above it read, COUPLES ONLY. But whatever sanitary facilities the building may once have had, none operated now. It was a reeking sty of filth and ordure.

Scores of wretched caravan slaves sprawled like dumb beasts of burden in the dim light of torches; the men and women to be sent as tribute to the Brotherhood of Diablo were sequestered beneath the dais.

Sword in hand, Derek flew the length of the building with the speed of a charging predator; but he could not outfly the startled gasps and cries all around him. These alerted the guards.

Their gnawed and pustulous faces gaped with such hideousness that Derek broke stride. But then they shrieked and bounded for the nearest exit. Slamming, banging, lunging again and again with all their weight at the steel doors, they could not open them. Their shrieks rose like the howls of trapped animals.

Again Derek recoiled from their hideousness. They carried truncheons with sharpened spikes at the end, and his hesitation emboldened them to attack. But they were thugs rather than true warriors, and Derek quickly overpowered them, although he felt that his sword was now utterly defiled. Cleaning it was not enough; he wanted to heat it in a fire.

Then he became aware of the commotion behind him, and he ran back into the midst of the caravan slaves with upraised arms, trying to quiet them. But they evidently thought that this was a victory gesture of some kind, and they cheered and shouted. It took several minutes to quiet them down.

But before he could speak he saw little Jana beckoning frantically from the door into the foyer. Then she glanced anxiously over her shoulder and disappeared. Derek raced for the door, his two pikemen behind him. They met the three returning guards head on.

This time he did not hesitate; nor did his pikemen. The fight was over in seconds, but now Derek did not stop even to clean his sword. How many other Children of Satan had been attracted by the commotion?

"Derek, over here!" came a voice behind him.

A single oil-lamp burned in the foyer, and at first he did not see Jana anywhere. Then she emerged from behind a row of lockers, with Buck right behind her.

"That's all," she said. "In fact, there's hardly anybody in the whole town now. But there are thousands. . . . Just a minute!" She tilted her little head to one side. "Maybe about a quarter mile from here, there are some people gathered. Fifteen or so. That way," she pointed.

"We're going there next. We need weapons, and that's where they're deposited. Under guard, unfortunately. Here, you men, start collecting these oil-lamps, and all the refill oil you can find."

There was no longer any problem in keeping the caravan slaves quiet; they realized now that it was their uproar which had attracted the guards, and they certainly did not want to attract any more. They were also less optimistic now about escaping. It took Derek several minutes to convince even the younger slaves that there really was a chance of getting away.

139

There was mutation and deformity, and their ancestors had belonged to several different races; but they were all now the mere pack animals of the Brotherhood of Diablo, tethered together for the night through the metal bands on their ankles. At last Derek stopped arguing and started cutting the ropes that bound them.

This should have inspired them; but instead they only leaped to their feet and began attacking each other. Or so it seemed. Then he realized that they were attacking just the men who sat at the head of each file. These were evidently the collaborators or jackals of the Brotherhood of Diablo. But it did settle the issue—there could be no turning back now.

He kept them in their original files until they had picked new leaders of their own. Mathew had already freed the tribute men and women, and was remonstrating with them. Apparently they just wanted to return to their home settlements, and he had to convince them that flight from the land was now their only hope of safety.

The costume of the Children of Satan was a kind of loose tunic, cut off at the shoulders to display their biceps, with tight leather trousers and heavy boots. Derek had his two pikemen strip the dead guards and don their costumes. It was still hard to see how anybody could consider them too beautiful, but he cautioned them to keep their helmets pulled forward and to stay in the shadows. They at last relinquished their pikes for the guards' truncheons.

Derek then picked a dozen of the younger caravan slaves, and led the way toward the makeshift armory. A wail of torment resounded eerily through the ruined town; then a wild explosion of thousands of voices, thundering their cheers. He did not have to encourage the rest of the escaping slaves to hurry in the opposite direction. He only hoped that they would not just keep running.

The lanterns that they carried burned a crude oil of some kind, but they cast a bright light, and he made sure that they were carefully hooded. Jana clung tightly to Buck's back, shivering at each wail of torment, at each explosion of thunderous cheering.

"Derek, wait!" she whispered suddenly. "I'm not sure, but I think . . ." She frowned in concentration. "There's about fifteen men gathered just ahead, but one of them seems different from the rest. Like Fatty, or that hairy nightmare that Eva killed in Saluston."

He thought for a moment. "It won't make any difference," he decided at last. "Fire is fire, even to the Brotherhood of Diablo. We'll just have to move a little faster, that's all."

The three-story brick building loomed just ahead, and he called everybody around him to make sure that they understood what they were supposed to do. Getting to the upper story would not be difficult; a stairway of metal rods covered the entire rear of the structure.

"Move fast," he added. "Just grab all you can carry and get out of town. You know where the others are waiting. Jana?"

"No change. They're all still on the ground floor, near the front of the building."

"All right, you'd better get moving, then. Go on, Buck! Go on, now!"

The huge beast glanced up at him with green saucer eyes, still half-shut against the bright moonlight, then turned reluctantly and padded off into the shadows. The caravan slaves seemed to relax—until the next wail of torment echoed through the streets.

Every window in the upper story was boarded over, but there was a skylight on the roof. Derek pried it open and dropped to the floor below. He unhooded his lantern and looked around. This had evidently been a public building of some kind, perhaps the town record office. Every wall was lined with wooden file cabinets. They would indeed have to move fast; the whole building was like a colossal torch just waiting to be lit.

He tiptoed into the corridor outside and peered over the bannister. The stairway was thick with dust, peeled wallpaper, and bits of fallen plaster, but otherwise unobstructed. Yellowed notices hung from an old bulletin board that caught his eye as he passed. A prominent notice lauding the use of nuclear power ended with a slogan in bold letters: THE ODDS AGAINST A MISHAP IN A NUCLEAR POWER PLANT ARE 1,000 TO 1. Somebody had scrawled beneath: *What are the odds when you build 1,000 nuclear power plants?*

He dragged a desk under the skylight, and the others climbed down. They worked fast, and soon the whole upper story reeked of lamp oil.

He hoisted the last of his men back up through the skylight and scrambled after him onto the roof. He waited until they had all reached the street below, then tossed a flaming lantern through the skylight and dived for the stairway. He gave the signal the instant his feet touched the ground.

"Fire! Fire!" cried his two pikemen, rushing to the front of the building.

A pillar of smoke, its base flecked with reddish light, already billowed from the roof above. Then all was pandemonium; shouting, cursing, rushing in and out the front door. The next reaction was naturally to see how serious the fire really was, and whether it could be extinguished. The weapons deposited on the ground floor were left unguarded for a few critical minutes.

Derek led the way around the front of the building. His pikemen waited on the threshold; and then they were all inside the door, snatching up armloads of swords, pikes, and shields. There were a few of the old firearms, but these were evidently just for display. At least, he hoped so.

Smoke was beginning to seep into the room, and the commotion upstairs grew more desperate. Any moment now the guards would realize that the building was doomed, that their efforts to stop the blaze were futile.

"Let's go!" cried Derek. "Just take what you've got!"

Most of his men were already gone, heavily laden with arms. The few that were still here had discovered some old blankets, and were tying the remaining weapons into large bundles. These were almost too heavy for them to carry. If they were pursued. . . .

A huge figure suddenly appeared at the top of the staircase. Derek snatched up a pike and hurled it at him. Despite his bulk, despite being caught utterly by surprise, his reflexes saved him from death. The pike caught him in the arm, rather than the heart, and he cried out something in anger.

For a moment Derek was astonished. Then he heard the whole nightmare contingent tumbling down from the smoke-filled upper story, and he raced for the door. He found his two pikemen waiting for him, and they hurried on together.

"All the men got out safe," they reported. "Nobody followed."

"They will soon," said Derek, glancing back toward the Place of Torment. "Thousands of them. Do you remember the place beyond the pass where we're to meet?" They repeated the directions accurately. "Good. Now get back to the sanctuary and tell Eva and Gunnar what's happened. They must leave at once."

"The bat-things?"

"It will be hours after midnight before you get back. The swarms of bat-things have never appeared so late at night. They must return to their own lairs before dawn. Now hurry!"

Derek trotted on alone through the crumbling ghost town. The huge figure that he had hurled his pike at was undoubtedly an agent of the Brotherhood of Diablo. It was not the creature's martial skill in evading a home thrust that had so astonished him. It was what he had cried out in anger: "Derek the Hunter!"

And yet this man had not been one of those who had invaded Saluston. How had he recognized him? Was the entire Brotherhood of Diablo now searching for him?

He crossed an open boulevard and overtook three men stumbling along with a bundle of weapons so heavy that they could hardly carry it. He took an end, and they cut through a silent, deserted building at the edge of town.

Weapons were already being distributed as they at last joined the others. Derek was relieved to find them all here. Then he noticed a group of people, including a number of the caravan slaves, kneeling together. Mathew stood facing them with his head bowed, holding his golden crucifix before him. It was evidently some kind of religious service.

CHAPTER 10: THE ENEMY FLANK

Rollo ignored the cries behind him; they were not very loud cries, nor even very determined. He knew that the message was important, although the men had ignored him completely while discussing it among themselves. But without Derek the Hunter leading the way, they crept along the mountain trail as if afraid that every shadow held some beast-thing just waiting to pounce on them.

But he was not afraid, and he plunged through the winding chain of cols, tracks, and defiles with the speed and certainty of Derek himself. If some beast-thing pounced—then it pounced. Although he could not resist a few nervous glances up at the sky.

The weird belling of dog-things echoed through the night as he at last approached the sanctuary, hours ahead of the others. He kept on running, until two dark figures suddenly emerged out of the shadows just ahead. They challenged him.

"Eva," he cried, panting for breath. "Important. A message from Derek the Hunter."

He was still breathing hard when she emerged from her room at the back of the cave. She was wearing hardly any clothes, and her voluptuous young body glistened like polished bronze in the torchlight. He had lately begun to find such things strangely fascinating, and for a few moments had trouble concentrating on the message from Derek. But at last he repeated it, word for word.

"Well done, Rollo," she said, smiling at him. "If you had stayed back with the others, you might have arrived too late." He threw back his shoulders with pride. "Now go wake your father."

His shoulders drooped again. "I was afraid of that," he muttered, and trudged back out of the cave.

At first he didn't know whether his father was going to pat his head or swat it. Apparently Gunnar didn't either, and the gesture fell somewhere in between.

Then Rollo was forgotten and apparently so were the swarms of bat-things. The full moon was halfway down the western sky, and soon the whole ragged, grumbling, whining, complaining, whimpering band was straggling in the same direction. But at least they were moving.

The pass lay only a few miles ahead; but it was uphill

all the way, and the eastern sky wore a ragged fringe of gray before they finally reached it. Eva had things well organized by then, especially the fighting men.

"There they are!" cried somebody, and a crowd of people ran forward to look.

"And there *they* are," muttered Gunnar, looking further out onto the plains, now a ghostly silver-white.

The band being led by Derek was about two miles away; it looked pathetically small compared to the horde pursuing them. All excitement died the moment these were seen.

"Two to one, maybe," Gunnar estimated. "Even if our fifty or sixty men join 'em, we'll still be outnumbered. Could be a bad fight. Real bad."

"Perhaps not," Eva said thoughtfully. "Not if we move with enough speed and audacity. I believe that's the rendezvous point they're heading for—that triangular group of hills?"

"That's it," Rollo blurted out. "Mathew described it, and I was listening and heard every word."

His father again rewarded him with something between a pat and a swat, and he stepped aside rubbing the back of his head.

At that moment the other messengers finally came straggling up, looking sheepish. They never got a chance to report.

"Heard it all, hours ago." Gunnar scowled at them. "I thought turtles were slow, but I had nothing to compare 'em with! Now there's going to be a fight, and those are our fighting men over there," he growled. "Since they're only about fifty yards away you should be able to join 'em within the next few hours—if you start now. Now, I said!''

They shot Rollo a dirty look as they scurried past toward the waiting troop. Meanwhile Eva organized the women and children so that they could move quickly forward in case of victory—or retreat just as quickly in case of defeat.

''We'd better hurry.'' Gunnar came shambling over to her with his great warclub. ''Derek's going to make his stand on those hills over there to the north, and he's going to need all the men he can get.''

''I'm thinking more about those low hills to the south.'' And she explained the principles of a flanking movement.

He gnawed his beard thoughtfully, then grinned. ''Yeah, that's pretty clever.''

''We must avoid a siege situation at all costs. Where's Stinky?''

''I'll get him.'' He shambled off, chuckling to himself. ''Pretty clever!''

But what he discovered as he approached the troop was not at all amusing. In the emergency of flight he had tended to overlook the condition of his men; if he responded at all to their complaints it was only with a growl or a cuff. Margo stood watching them as if they were so many insects under a magnifying glass.

''The variations observable in the abstinence syndrome . . .''

Gunnar shambled past her without paying any attention. First of all, he rarely knew what she was talking about; secondly, and most important of all, Derek and his men had almost reached the triangular group of hills.

''I told you chuckleheads to leave them pomegranates

alone," he growled. "But you wouldn't listen. Well, you'll listen now, or I'll know the reason why. Understand?"

He menaced them like an angry bear-thing risen onto its hind legs, and most of the men decided that they were not really as nauseous as they had thought. There were yawns and sneezes, coughs and chattering teeth, but they shuffled into ranks, ready to go down onto the plains and fight the Children of Satan. Their only alternative was even grimmer—to stay here and fight Gunnar.

"All right, Hobie," he growled. "Up on your feet and in the ranks with the others."

The man was in a pathetic condition, shivering and sweating at the same time, panting for breath as if he were being suffocated, doubled up with cramps. Gunnar tried to put him on his feet, but his mere touch caused the man to cry out in pain.

"I can't make it now, Gunnar," he whined. "Go on ahead, and I'll catch up with you in a few minutes. I promise."

"The wretch is patently inefficacious for any martial enterprise," said Margo. "But consigned to my observation, his convulsive lancinations may yet remunerate us with data."

She sat on a rock and peered coldly down at the man, writhing and moaning on the ground before her in the agonies of withdrawal. Gunnar shrugged helplessly, and turned away. He collared Stinky.

"We need you to take a message, but you'll have to move fast."

"Don't m-move no other way."

He sent him off to Eva, and explained to his men what

151

they were going to do and why they were going to do it. They too seemed to think that it was pretty clever.

"Eva has many brilliant ideas," said one man in admiration, and the entire troop nodded in agreement.

Gunnar lowered on them. "And what makes you think that the idea couldn't have been mine?"

Nobody said anything.

"They're all up there on the pass, Derek," said Jana, sliding from Buck's back.

Their forced march across the plains had been only light exercise to the great beast; but he sensed the approach of dawn, and crept beneath a dark thicket and closed his eyes.

The pass was a good two miles away, and at first Derek could not see anybody there. Nor did he have time to look very closely. They were outnumbered two to one, and he hurriedly arranged his men to repel the first assault. An uphill charge against a phalanx of pikemen might discourage any attacking force, assuming that they attacked at all. The Children of Satan could only grow stronger by waiting. They now numbered in the hundreds, and they had thousands more in reserve, perhaps already moving in this direction.

Then he saw a troop of some fifty or sixty armed men descending from the pass. But his elation was quickly dashed—they were going the wrong way! He watched with dismay as they disappeared behind some low hills to the south.

"Here comes Stinky!" cried Jana.

With a gait that seemed to cover ten feet at a stride, the

long-legged Newcome lad flew toward them across the plains. The Children of Satan, massing at the foot of the hill, also saw him coming. But he was past them before the orders were even given to try and intercept him. He was not even winded.

"Eva said I should t-tell you that Gunnar's agoing to t-take 'em in the f-f-flank. Which means, I g-guess, from the side. And you're to charge d-down at 'em the minute Gunnar hits. But you shouldn't pursue. Which m-means, I guess, to chase 'em."

Derek smiled somewhat wryly. Eva's study of military science had left him far behind in the effective handling of troops in the face of the enemy, even more so in the principles of strategy. Massing all available men here on the hilltop would surely have led to disaster; he saw that now. Their objective was a strategic retreat from the country, not the winning of a meaningless battle, which would only give the main body of the enemy time to come up in force.

Nor did he send Eva any advice now about mobilizing the rest of their own people. His old habits of thinking died hard, but he was learning.

"I want to send a message back to Eva. Can you do some more running?"

"Rather do that than stay here and f-fight," said Stinky.

"All right, just tell her that I agree with her tactics."

He nodded. "Does seem p-pretty clever, when you think about it." Then he threw back his little round head and vanished in a blur of arms and legs.

"Throw rocks at them," cried Derek. "Anything you can find. Keep them looking this way."

The barrage of rocks and debris indeed held the attention of those massing below, and they cursed and shook their weapons defiantly. Even little Jana threw a stone, but it only hit one of their own men in the back of the head. He whirled angrily around; but she was already looking innocently in another direction.

Derek meanwhile summoned his captains around him. They all realized by now that they would never survive a single day, besieged here on an open hilltop. It did not take him long to convince them that a determined charge was their best hope of victory. Refraining from pursuit was more difficult to explain.

"We must be out of the country before nightfall. Mathew here tells me that there is a mountain lake about fifteen miles—"

"The Devil's Bridge!" cried one of the local men, but even some of the caravan slaves seemed to know what he was talking about. "No man knows where it comes from or where it leads. Not even the Children of Satan go there."

"So I'm told," said Derek. The structure was supposed to be the passageway of the Devil, a huge sealed vault, supported by arches, that ran from one mountain to the next. He thought he knew what it was, an ideal passage into the west—provided that it was uninhabited. "We must reach this lake before nightfall—" There was a tug at his sleeve and he bent down to listen.

Jana whispered, "Gunnar and the others are getting close. I don't think those maggot-faces down there have seen them yet."

"All right, men," cried Derek. "Let's take our positions." He drew his sword and strode to the front of the phalanx, his back turned contemptuously toward the enemy massed below. "Now do all you men in the front rank have two pikes? Don't hurl them until you're almost to the bottom of the hill, when you're charging full speed. You'll have more power then. Here, give me one of those." He hefted the stout pike, and turned to face the enemy. "Begin at a walk. Don't charge until I give the signal."

The full moon was low in the western sky, and the silvery plain was now fading into a cold, sickly gray. He was glad that there was no more light than there was—the faces of the enemy would not be visible until it was too late to turn back. Angry shouts and turmoil erupted below as he led his troop at a walk down the hillside.

Then a cry somewhere between a growl and a bellow sounded off to the left, and a huge bearlike form charged straight into the enemy flank. Derek sounded his own battle cry, and led the charge down the hillside, hurling his pike with all his force just before he reached the bottom. It impaled the enemy directly in front of him, driving him backwards into the rank behind. Scores of pikes now flew into the ranks of the enemy. Their confusion was utter. Derek drew his sword and dived at the throat of a maggot-faced horror.

Confused, demoralized, seemingly attacked on all sides at once, the Children of Satan never rallied from the first shock. They threw down their weapons and broke, but even this did not save them. More died trying to run away than had been killed in the battle itself. The victory was overwhelming.

Derek leaped, dodged, and raced out onto the plain,

quickly outdistancing pursued and pursuers alike. But the moment he was in front of the foremost of his own troop, he slid to a halt and whirled around, arms upraised and shouting:

"Let them go! No pursuit! There's no time!"

Nor was there any chance now that the surviving Children of Satan would rally. Less than half their original number had been able to run from the battlefield, and they kept on running. The base of the hill was strewn with the dead and the dying.

Derek at last managed to halt the pursuit; although the fury of vengeance, the bitter memories of long years of torment and suffering, were not easily quelled. But it was too late to halt his men from avenging themselves on the wounded. There were no prisoners.

"I think I'll boil my warclub," said Gunnar, coming over to him. "Their blood is red, although you'd expect it to be green, by the looks of 'em."

Derek cleaned his own sword, plunging it again and again into the sandy earth to remove its taint. Maybe he would boil it along with Gunnar's warclub.

CHAPTER 11: The Devil's Bridge

The rest of their people were already straggling up by the time Derek and Gunnar returned to the hillside. Eva had apparently mobilized them the instant the battle turned in their favor.

Derek met her eyes, and he knew that she had already examined him for any wound or injury. But they were still a long day's march from safety; each knew what had to be done, and they went about their respective duties with mutual confidence and respect. It was now full morning, and the corpses of the Children of Satan were a ghastly sight indeed.

Margo obviously approved of the slaughter of the captives and wounded, but she realized that Jana was watching her narrowly, ready to pounce on any cold-blooded observation that she might make. So she did her observing in silence, moving curiously among the hideous corpses as if they were mere biological specimens.

"A sodalitive precursor of the socio-economic control of the Brotherhood of Diablo," she announced at last. "I had assumed as much—an easily predicted instance of the weaker reflecting the mores of the more puissant. A biological imperative, if you will."

Gunnar stared down at her in wonder, as if he still could not make her out. "Whatever that means, I think we'd better get moving. If these beauties catch us out in the open we'll be in a bad way." He winked at Margo. "Even I can figure that one out, kid."

"They will not approach within miles of the Devil's Bridge," Mathew assured them. "If we can avoid ambush til then, we may be safe. Except," he added, "for the bridge itself."

Was the Devil's Bridge inhabited? Since nature seemed to be desperately trying to refill all its old, shattered niches, that was certainly a possibility. And if this huge sealed vault ran from one mountain to another, what might be in the mountains themselves? The last time they had tried to enter the mountains, they had been savagely attacked by ape-things. Derek described the incident.

"Squashies?" cried Mathew, looking very concerned indeed. "So close to us? I have heard that they were multiplying in mountain districts, that they have even raided outlying settlements of the Children of Satan. But so close?'' He seemed more relieved than ever to have fled his small sanctuary. "They might have been a menace to stragglers or even a small party, but we are too many for them now."

"Let's hope none of us see any more of them."

Derek found Eva and explained to her all that he had heard about the Devil's Bridge, and what he thought it really was. It could be a grave danger; but it might also mean their salvation.

"Torches?" she exclaimed. "Yes, I see what you mean. How far do you think it leads?"

"Perhaps only a few miles. Perhaps through the entire mountain range. The longer the better."

There had been few casualties in the battle, none killed; and all but four of the wounded still ambulatory. Most were now confident of their safe passage out of the country. But Derek himself was not quite so confident, although he kept such doubts to himself. Whatever spur was needed for a vigorous and rapid pursuit would be provided by the agents of the Brotherhood of Diablo. They now knew that he was here. . . .

There was some grumbling at midday; the plains behind them seemed empty, and the people had been on the march since well before dawn. But Derek kept them moving. Not only the wounded but most of the smaller children now had to be carried. Hobie was in a desperate condition.

"Look at the poor wreck," said Gunnar. "His skin looks like a plucked bird-thing."

Even getting men to carry Hobie was a problem. Not only was he sweating and chattering with cold, but he was also incontinent. The caravan slaves refused to touch him. At last the men from the sanctuary assumed the unpleasant duty out of charity.

"See what the rest of you chuckleheads would be like by now, if I'd let you go on eating them pomegranates," Gunnar growled. "I told you and I told you, but you wouldn't listen." He shambled away shaking his head in disgust.

The dry wisps of cloud high overhead gave little protection from the afternoon sun; bunch grass and stunted thorn bushes were the only vegetation, and great-winged carrion birds wheeled through the heat risers above them. At last somebody spotted a dust cloud directly behind them, and Derek no longer had to encourage the people to keep moving. Then they had to make an unexpected detour.

The playa itself had dried to a few shallow pools, and was solid enough to cross. But here and there were ominous black holes about the diameter of a man's body.

"Terrible snake-things," Mathew warned them. "As big around as a man, and nobody knows how long. When the lake is filled, they feed on the creatures that come here to drink. But it is dry now, and they are hungry."

"There's a lot of nasty things down there, all right," said Jana. "We're already closer than I'd like to be."

Derek glanced back across the plains. The dust cloud that they had first seen on the horizon, about two hours ago, was closer now. Perhaps miles closer.

"How far do they stretch from their holes?" asked Derek.

Mathew consulted a man whose settlement was nearby before answering. "Twenty feet, sometimes thirty. But when the lake dries like this they have been known to leave their holes altogether in search of food. We have no choice but to detour.''

Margo peered intently at the nearest hole, which was less than two hundred feet away. Jana sidled toward her, obviously about to make a suggestion of some kind. But Derek set her firmly on Buck before she could say anything, and led the way due north.

They lost over an hour circling the playa, and the dust cloud veered toward them like an oncoming predator. Then they were into rough country; the land grew steeper and rockier, and they lost even more time. But there was no more grumbling; the people had seen the dust cloud, and they knew what it meant. More and more of the great carrion birds wheeled slowly overhead, as if they too understood the meaning of the approaching dust cloud.

Meanwhile Eva kept the women and older children occupied in gathering and plaiting material for torches. They had made hundreds by the time they reached the old mountain road, from which they quickly dug up basketfuls of tar.

"There is the lake," said Mathew, pointing down from the side of the road. "And there—you can just see it through the windgap to the west—there is the Devil's Bridge."

"What's that stone structure out on the lake?"

"The Devil's Castle. You can see where his bridge enters the dark realm beneath the mountain. This must all seem very strange to you."

"No, I once saw something like it in a book illustration.

Jana, I think there's somebody down there. Those look like small boats of some kind.''

She was silent for several moments, as the people continued to straggle wearily past them toward the Devil's Bridge. A couple of the ambulatory wounded had finally collapsed, and now they too had to be carried. Hobie was so foul and wretched that he seemed barely human, and soon there was no point in carrying him any further.

"Lots of things down there," Jana said at last. "Humans, beast-things, some a little of both. Mostly by that stone structure, but also all along that big tube that's half out of the water, and right into the mountain.''

"How far into the mountain?" Derek cried apprehensively.

She concentrated; then slowly shook her head. "Hard to tell exactly, but pretty deep. I think we've got them outnumbered, though. Unless there's a lot of them so deep in the mountain that I can't find them at all.''

Derek glanced back across the plain. "Let's keep moving.''

The gorge between the gray-brown mountain walls was only about a hundred feet deep; its stream in no place reached as high as the knees. Slender arches of reinforced concrete supported the huge enclosed vault overhead; it stretched directly from one mountain wall to the other.

"Empty," said Jana. "Everybody's in the direction of the lake. But the mountains the other way are so big that it's hard to tell. I hope we don't run into a mob of Gunks, way underground.''

"Held my weight," said Gunnar, returning from a test of the concrete stairs that ran up to the vault overhead.

"But maybe we'd better not put too many people on it at once. How much time do we have, small stuff?"

"Couple of hours, I'd guess," said Jana. "They're still miles away. But we've got hundreds of people to get through—how big is the door?"

"It's not a door, just a round metal cover at the top of the vault. Got some men working on it now."

"What do you mean?" cried Derek.

"Seems to be stuck from the inside."

Margo nodded, as if she had expected just such a contingency. "This vault is patently an extension of the similar structure emanating from the stone edifice in yonder lake. Its inhabitants have prudently obviated access from a quarter not readily defensible. In short, they've locked their back door."

"Margo, if just once in your life—" Jana began impatiently.

"Can't budge it, Gunnar," one of his men called down. "Shakes a little, but it won't open."

"Shakes a little!" he growled. "There'll be more than a little shaking when I get up there. Here, gimme that pike. No, the thick metal one. That's right."

His men had prudently sidled out of reach by the time he had climbed up onto the enclosed vault. The metal cover was just loose enough to wedge the tip of the pike under it. Gunnar spit on his hands, grabbed the handle, and heaved. There was a sharp hollow snap, and the cover flew open with a clang.

"Shakes a little!" he said disgustedly, tossing away the bent pike. "Just let me get my paws on one of you chuckleheads, and I'll show you what shaking really is. This'll teach me to send boys to do a man's job.''

''Still empty,'' said Jana, as Derek set her down. ''Whew! Don't smell very good, though. What is this thing anyway?''

Derek replied, ''Remember the book about ancient Rome that I read to you and Eva a couple of years ago?''

''*Quo* something-or-other?''

''*Quo Vadis*. There was an illustration in the book of a structure something like this. It's called an aqueduct. It carries water over a long distance.'' He signaled down to Eva, who started the people up the stairway, careful not to overload it.

''I don't see any water,'' said Jana, peering into the opening. ''There's a ladder, though.''

''Let's test it,'' said Derek. He was down and back up again in a few moments. ''Solid as a rock. Better start lighting some of those torches. You can squeeze in there, can't you, Gunnar?''

''Don't worry about me.'' He took one of the torches and lowered himself through the opening. ''Start sending the rest of 'em down.''

Months of hardship, danger, and rigorous adaptation to the wilderness of the sun since their flight from Saluston had hardened the people. There was neither panic nor even reluctance as they descended one by one into the aqueduct. The caravan slaves had been heartened by their victory over the Children of Satan, and they were no longer as abject as they had been. It was the tribute men and women who showed the most anxiety. After all, this was the bridge used by the Devil to pass between his dark realms under the mountains. But even they were at last coaxed down the ladder.

"Buck!" cried Jana. "We forgot Buck! How is he going to get down there?"

But the great beast had no trouble at all. He bounded up the concrete stairs the moment Derek called, and leaped up onto the vault, although not once did he seem to open his eyes. Derek helped Jana down the ladder, and they both looked up and called. Then the light disappeared as Buck poked his shaggy head into the opening. Two big green lights flashed through the dark, and he was sitting beside them.

A piece of rusty pipe had been used to bar the the metal cover from the inside. Derek replaced it with a pair of solid metal pikes. It would now be easier to cut through the concrete vault itself than to open this cover again.

The sound of hundreds of shuffling feet echoed through the vault, which was about twelve feet in diameter; the people were already too far ahead for torchlight to reach this far back. Two green saucer eyes glowed softly in the dark.

"We'll bring up the rear," said Derek, taking Jana's hand. "I'm more worried about what might be sneaking up behind us than what's ahead."

"Nothing so far," said Jana. "But this has to come out somewhere. Won't the Brotherhood of Diablo be waiting for us?"

"Not if this aqueduct continues to run due west. Both Mathew and the caravan slaves that I checked with say that anybody trying to follow us would have to detour hundreds of miles around the mountains. And there's no water to slow us down.''

"Why not? Isn't that what this thing was built for—to carry water?''

"That stone structure out in the lake was probably the pumping station. But the pumps are off now.''

"What if somebody turns them back on?''

Derek was silent for a long moment. "Just keep walking,'' he said at last.

CHAPTER 12: THE PUMPING STATION

"Nothing's collapsed, far as I can see," said Gunnar, holding up his torch. "Looks almost like somebody tried to build a wall."

"I think that's just what it is," said Derek. "A wall."

Brick and concrete rubble packed the vault of the aqueduct so tightly that not even a pike could be wedged through. It was rough work, although there was soon little doubt that it was man-made. But who had built it, and why? What lay on the other side? There was no point in asking Jana: she was still unable to find anything so deep beneath the mountains.

"There was one of them metal covers about a half mile back," said Gunnar.

He did not have to say anything more. Their hopes of just marching securely down the aqueduct until they reached some refuge in the west had literally banged into a wall. It was fortunate that one of the metal covers was so close at hand. There were stretches over the last two days when they had marched for hours without seeing one.

"Why can't we take Buck?" cried Jana, as she watched Derek scale the ladder. "There might be trouble, or we might have to run fast."

"Got any ideas how we might get him up to that hole in the ceiling?" said Gunnar. "I'll be lucky if I can get up there myself."

Jana had to content herself with hugging Buck and scratching his ears. She did not at all like the idea of leaving him behind when there was possible danger—where she might find herself left behind. Nor had she any illusions about her own prowess in a fight.

"Not even locked," Derek shouted down. There was a tortured groan of metal as he pried open the cover. "Looks like it's going to rain."

"What's that above you?" Gunnar called up to him.

"Just what we're looking for—a highway bridge."

Another ladder rose to the highway span above, and soon the entire reconnoitering party was assembled in the midafternoon murkiness. A fine drizzle, almost a mist, was now beginning to fall.

"Mountain weather, all right," said Mathew. "Doubt if we'll get much rain, though. Only this mizzly stuff."

But Derek was more interested right now in Jana's

reaction to their surroundings. She seemed unhappier than ever about leaving Buck behind.

"This highway will only lead us straight into trouble," she said. "Big trouble. There couldn't be more nasty things straight ahead if they were all just sitting there waiting for us."

"The Children of Satan?"

"No, no, Derek," Mathew answered for her. "We are now well beyond their territory."

The two caravan slaves, who might also be expected to know something about these parts, nodded in agreement. More important, Jana herself agreed.

"I think it might be the Brotherhood of Diablo themselves," she reported. "About a dozen or so, and I don't know how many of those bigfoot uglies. Some of them must be even dumber than the ones we ran into before."

"How far away?"

"Half a mile, maybe less. They're all camped close together without even sentries just beyond where the highway bends around that ridge." She frowned. "Couldn't we build some kind of ramp for Buck? It probably wouldn't take very long."

"I think you'd better just go back down and keep him company yourself. There's nothing more that you can do here."

"Well, if you're sure you don't need me . . ." She vanished before he could change his mind.

"You don't need me either, Derek," said Gunnar. "Looks like we'll have to get through downstairs somehow, and I'd better get 'em started right now." He shook his head wearily. "First it's hedges, and now a wall. What next?"

Derek kept only the two caravan slaves with him, and sent the others back down with Gunnar. There was no need of further reconnaissance. Jana had answered every question for them. Or, perhaps, all but one. Why were agents of the Brotherhood of Diablo encamped with ape-things so close to where the aqueduct was walled off below?

The misty rain continued to fall as the three jogged down the old highway. Jana had not found any sentries, so there was no need for concealment until they reached the actual ridge overlooking the camp. But all they saw at first were the ruins of an ugly sprawl of concrete buildings, surrounded by rusty barbed-wire fence.

Only now did Derek explain fully what they were looking for to the caravan slaves, who still thought that Jana was only a little girl, a kind of mascot. They seemed to understand at once what it was all about.

"They camp now to get out of the rain," said one of them. "I have heard about such hunts."

"Yes," added the other, "the Invincibles hunt only the largest and most powerful for breeding. Some of the wild ones are almost as big as Mogs already."

"Mogs? *Almost* as big?" cried Derek. "One of those that I saw was a good seven and a half feet tall. Mathew called them Squashies."

"I've heard that name too," said the first caravan slave. "But the Mogs are bigger and more terrible, over nine feet high and much heavier than the wild ones. Nothing can stand against them."

"They say that the Rathagon has a bodyguard of a hundred Mogs," added the second slave. "I have heard many terrible stories about what is done in the chambers beneath the Rath of Diablo."

"We'll talk about that later," said Derek. Rain or no rain, it was still possible that the agents of the Brotherhood of Diablo had been told that he and the others had fled through the aqueduct, and were waiting for them here. As far as he could determine, the underground tunnel ran very close to this ugly sprawl of concrete buildings, perhaps directly below it. "Wait here," he said, "I want a closer look for myself."

There were several gaps in the barbed-wire fence, and he had no trouble reaching the nearest building unseen. But it was roofless and deserted, and he crept on to the next. This was the largest structure of the entire complex. Over its stone entrance facade were engraved the words: HARRISON B. SMALLEY PUMPING AND FILTRA-TION PLANT. This building was definitely not deserted; although even here there was not a single guard or sentinel.

He had wanted a closer look—and one look was all he needed. Nor was it something he ever forgot. That the bigfooted ape-things might ever appear small was something that had never occurred to him; they now seemed almost puny beside the creatures towering ominously beside each of them, silent and watchful. They showed no inclination even to try and escape.

The agents of the Brotherhood of Diablo were more huge and gruesome than any he had seen thus far; each was different in his own terrible way, as if all the most hideous changelings spawned by the cataclysm had banded together to avenge themselves on nature, or upon the last defenseless survivors of the world that had been. Three great roasting spits bore the carved remains of an unnatural feast.

The narrow ledge ran all the way around the second story, and Derek crept to the next window for a better perspective. No, there were only two means of descent to whatever lay beneath the structure; both walled off with brick and concrete rubble, just as in the aqueduct below. This could only be a hunting party, after all; their presence here merely a coincidence.

This part of the ledge was exposed to the misty rain, and he edged very cautiously back toward the overhanging tree. To slip and fall now could only mean ending up on the next roasting spit.

By the time he and the two caravan slaves were safely back inside the aqueduct, Gunnar had begun work on the wall of rubble. His brigade had already cleared several courses near the ceiling.

"No metal tools, Gunnar," Derek cautioned him, explaining what he had seen directly above. "It all has to be done by hand, and no loud talking or shouting."

"But what's behind this wall?" Gunnar whispered.

"We'll know when we get through it."

The courses of brick and concrete rubble seemed endless, and hours passed before Gunnar could at last stretch a flaming torch through a narrow fissure and peer beyond the wall. He raised his eyebrows in perplexity.

"Nothing," he grumbled. "Nothing at all. It's just a big vaulted tunnel like the one we're in now."

"They're still there," Jana reported back, after being sent up on the highway bridge again. "It's dark outside now, but it's still drizzling."

Derek sighed, "Then they've settled down for the night. Let's get this wall down, and as far away from here as we can before morning. We can't be many days march from the end of this aqueduct.''

Derek strode down the deep tunnel with a fresh torch, examining the ceiling every step of the way. What he saw could only reassure him of their safety. If the Brotherhood of Diablo was so resolute in their search for machines that they would send their agents all the way to Saluston, they obviously could not suspect what lay beneath the ugly sprawl of concrete buildings above. Here were the most colossal machines that he had ever seen in his life. But there were also gaping holes in the floor above through which the least sound might be magnified as through the aperture of a musical instrument.

How thick were the walls blocking descent from the upper stories? Thick enough to block sound from below? It may have taken his own people hours to get through the wall, but the Mogs looked like they could tear their way through the same thickness in minutes.

He beckoned to Jana.

"I can find them now," she whispered. "But just barely. These walls make it harder to find things than even in Saluston."

"Probably some special kind of reinforced concrete." He held up his torch. "Do you think you could manage that ladder over there, or would you rather sit on my shoulder?"

"Well, if we have to go up there at all, I suppose I'd rather let you do the climbing. That ladder must be two stories high."

At that moment Gunnar came shuffling up to them, frowning and gnawing his beard in frustration. "Another wall! Same as the one we just pulled down—maybe even thicker. And what if there's more beyond that?''

Derek shook his head. ''I doubt that we'll run into any more obstacles. At least, man-made obstacles. Whoever used this old pumping station as a refuge probably just sealed off all its entrances against attack. By whom or what, we don't know.''

''What if they're still there?'' Gunnar looked uneasily at the gaping hole above him. ''How about it, small stuff?''

Jana shook her head. ''Nobody's there.''

''We're going to stay up there while the tunnel is being cleared, to make sure it stays that way,'' said Derek. ''No more noise than you can help, Gunnar.''

He nodded. ''I'll keep everybody back, except the lads doing the actual work. Might even be a good idea to move 'em all the way back to that opening, so we can get 'em out of here in case of trouble. I don't want to get caught down here by them big hairy brutes you told us about.''

Derek did not bother to add that their chances would not be much better out in the open. Gunnar was certainly right about their having no chance at all if they were caught down here. The agents of the Brotherhood of Diablo would not hesitate to change the nature of their hunt.

With Jana perched securely on his shoulder, he climbed the narrow metal ladder to the floor above. Flame pinwheeled through the air, and a torch landed on the concrete floor beside him. He snatched it up; then stood aside while three unlighted torches were also tossed up from below, to be used when the first burned out.

''I don't think even the Brotherhood of Diablo could

budge these machines," whispered Jana. "Look how tall they are. I didn't know we were so far underground."

"I didn't either," Derek replied, "but the farther the better. I think that must be one of the stairways I saw from above."

They crept silently between the towering rows of machines, looming monstrously above them in the trembling light of the torch. Derek wondered which was ultimately the most significant—the technology that could build such marvelous devices, or the technology that could destroy the world they were built to serve. Perhaps it was the same thing.

"There's a big thick door up there," whispered Jana. "And you say there's a thick wall on the other side?" She was silent a moment. "Then why am I whispering? They can't possibly hear us."

"They can't see us either." Derek lighted a candle stub he found propped in a tiny metal tray. "Wait here, I'm going to tell the others."

"Don't you think we should do some more exploring first?" she said innocently. "I don't think we ought to take chances, until we're absolutely sure what's up here."

He looked curiously at her, wondering what she was up to; but then she burst into a merry laugh.

"Besides," she added, "the longer we stay up here, the less work we'll have to do down in the tunnel."

"Wait here," said Derek.

Gunnar listened to him as he called down through the gap in the tunnel ceiling.

"It's about time we got a break," he grumbled. "We can use metal tools now, and get the job done in half the

175

time. No sense sending everybody back up the tunnel any more either.''

"You might send some of them up here," said Derek. "I found one candle, there may be more. Also, we're running low on torches. Maybe we can find the materials to make some more.''

Eva was the first person to climb the ladder. She had kept the women and older children busy plaiting torches all during their march down the aqueduct. But the necessary materials were all gone now, and she was even more concerned than Derek about their dwindling number of torches. She brought her ten best workers along with her.

The people huddled very close together as they crept timidly along behind Derek and Eva. Then all at once they heard a wail in the distance, and tiny footsteps rushing toward them. A moment later the terrified Jana burst into the light, and straight into Eva's arms.

"They're moving!" she cried. "They're dead, but they're moving! Just like those fossil things in the valley.''

"The rest of you get back to the ladder," said Derek, drawing his sword. "Jana, show me where they are.''

"Oh, all right. I just wish Buck could climb ladders too," she muttered, reluctantly leading the way back through the rows of towering machines. "There're six of them, but they must have all been asleep. I opened a door, there was a whoosh of air, and I saw these six people lying on a long table. Then all of a sudden they began shaking, like they were getting ready to jump up and chase me. There's the door," she whispered, hanging back.

Six humans—a woman and five children, ranging in age from about eight to perhaps sixteen or seventeen—were laid out in a row in what seemed to be some kind of storage room for supplies and machine parts. The bodies twitched spasmodically as they decayed before Derek's very eyes.

Then he recalled the shoosh of air that Jana had mentioned, and examined the door. It was hermetically sealed. This was the first air to attack the corpses in generations, and the processes of decay had resumed explosively. He found a stack of coarse woolen blankets and covered them one by one.

He also found a crate filled with wax candles, and hauled it outside. At least they would not continue their march down the aqueduct in total darkness. There were also more stacks of blankets—something the refugees always seemed to be in short supply of—as well as buckets of tar and grease, and wooden dowels that might be cut or broken into suitable lengths.

Jana's nature was too happy and resilient to be terrified about anything very long, and she skipped along beside Derek as he searched for other useful supplies. But she was still chary about opening strange doors. The next supply room they entered was definitely not hermetically sealed.

"Ugh, what a mess!" cried Jana. "It looks like the whole place exploded. Although I think it must have been a long time ago."

"We've seen this before," said Derek. "People use to preserve their food in metal containers, but after a while these would swell up and sometimes explode. There's nothing here we can use."

At last they came to what must have been the living

quarters of the people who had taken refuge here, perhaps during or immediately after the cataclysm. Sleeping rooms had been roughly partitioned off from a large central living room over fifty feet long. It was comfortably furnished and cluttered with an amazing array of toys and games.

"Oh, I've seen those before too," said Jana. "Those black boxes with the knobs on top."

"Yes, they're called storage batteries. They were used to provide energy to run machines or to light things." Derek examined the long row of batteries, their terminals connected in series by thick cables. Then he held up his torch and examined the ceiling; lighting fixtures hung in several places, all attached by wires to the row of batteries. "Nothing much here that we can use."

"How about those books over there, Derek. There must be hundreds of them, all made out of paper."

He only had time for a quick glance. None of the titles of the paperback books was familiar to him; the pages were so brown and brittle that they were barely legible. Then he heard an odd sound behind him and turned around.

"There was a green table with a net across the middle just like this one at Saluston," said Jana, bouncing the little white ball up and down. "But there were no paddles or balls like this. It's a game of some kind, isn't it?"

"Yes, but games are something we have no time for now." He glanced wistfully toward the stacks of paperbacks, knowing that he could not take them with him. "Oh, hello, Rollo. Did your father send you?"

The boy nodded. "He said to tell you that there's only open tunnel as far as he can see on the other side of the wall, and that the last of it will be down in about twenty minutes or so, and that we'd all better get ready to move.''

"All right,'' said Derek, "we'll all go down together. I think we've got about everything we want up here.''

"Except one thing,'' said Jana. "We don't know who laid out all those bodies in that supply room. They didn't do it themselves, and every entrance to this place is sealed. By the way, what do you think killed them all at the same time?''

"My guess is that sickness that the old-timers told us about. People who weren't injured in any way by the cataclysm would just sicken and die for no obvious reason. It had something to do with poisons radiating through the air, I believe.''

"Derek,'' cried Eva, hurrying up, "I found something. It's not very pretty.''

He followed her back to where two ramps crossed high overhead. It was indeed not very pretty; in fact, reconstructing events, it must have been tragic. Unlike the corpses in the supply room, this one was desiccated until it was little more than a skeleton.

"Both legs are broken,'' said Eva.

Derek glanced at the ramps above. "It looks like he fell, and then tried to drag himself away.'' He wondered how many months or years the man had survived here alone after the death of the rest of his family. "Now we know who laid out the other bodies.''

"They must have tried to build a refuge here, like Saluston. Except after the cataclysm, instead of before. We'll never go back to living underground, will we?''

"Never, if I can help it. Man was meant to live in the

sunlight, and that's where we're going now, forever. Gunnar's almost through the wall.''

As he hurried back to pick up Jana and Rollo, he heard a steady ping-pong-ping-pong sound, growing louder as he approached. Reluctantly, they laid down their paddles and followed him back between the rows of towering machines. The last of Eva's people were even now handing down their last armloads of blankets and fresh torches.

"I just thought of something, Derek," said Jana, skipping along beside him. "Why did these poor people here build walls down in the aqueduct in the first place? It must have been a lot of work for them. Maybe there's something down there that we don't know about."

"If there is, it can't be any worse than what's camped in the building above."

Jana did not say anything more.

Chapter 13: The Wise Woman

Derek exhausted food, torches, and people in his urgency to reach the mouth of the aqueduct. But such speed turned out to be unnecessary. Even if the Brotherhood of Diablo had somehow been alerted to their coming, they could hardly have been waiting for them at the mouth of the aqueduct. They probably did not even know of its existence. It opened at the bottom of the sea.

"No wonder we didn't run into anything down here." Gunnar stared despondently down at the water lapping about his feet. "It's uphill all the way back, and we're almost out of food."

"Take the torches away," said Derek, cupping his hands beside his eyes like blinkers. "Yes, you can see light. Fairly bright, too. The opening can't be very far underwater."

"Never work," said Gunnar, shaking his head. "Hardly any of these folks can swim at all, let alone that far underwater. I know I can't."

"Well, maybe if I swam out there, and perhaps rigged lines of some sort. . . ."

"Why don't you just wait?" said Margo. "Pedestrian departure is infinitely to be preferred to any manner of natatory egress. The water's briny sapidity, in conjunction with an evident lack of profluence beyond its current procerity, counsels patience. In short, the tide will turn."

While Gunnar blinked at her in wonder and Jana fumed, Derek knelt and tasted the water. He nodded. It was the sea all right; they had evidently arrived at high tide. But if the waters now blocked their way, they also protected them. There was no way of knowing what dangers lurked outside the aqueduct; if they just waited for the tide to ebb, it would then be too late to retreat to safety if something hostile was indeed waiting for them.

Nor was it prudent to go alone. Were he attacked, he might not be able to get back to warn the others; and even a few hours headstart might be enough to discourage casual pursuit. Nothing would help them, of course, if the whole Brotherhood of Diablo was waiting for them outside, ready to pounce.

The people had learned many skills since leaving Saluston, but swimming was not one of them. There was only one person who had learned to swim well enough to accompany him now. Eva needed just a few seconds to strip off the bits of fur that were her only clothing. They waded naked through the water until it reached their chests, then plunged beneath.

The light was farther away than he had thought, and he was encumbered by his sword; he began to wonder if the mouth of the aqueduct was ever completely out of water, even at low tide. Silver-blue fish darted out of their way as they at last reached the end of the tunnel.

A thin line rasped Derek's forearm as he rose toward the light, and an oddly twisted worm jerked convulsively past his ear. Then he and Eva broke the surface. They shook the water out of their eyes and blinked at the bright sunlight, but before they could start for shore, they realized that they were not alone.

The aqueduct stretched like a concrete pier out into the waters of a shallow sea; only the keystone of the arched vaulting around its mouth was visible above the surface. There sat a man with a fishing pole. He looked very surprised indeed.

The ruggedness of the coastline indicated that it had only recently been formed; storm beaches alternated with sea stacks of black basalt as far as the eye could see in either direction; there were few patches of smooth land. The mountain range rising behind the coast showed signs of recent convulsions. The aqueduct continued in the form of an open concrete channel out beneath the sea.

"Who are you?" said Derek, keeping his sword hidden under the water.

The man's only response was to drop his fishing pole as if it had just stung him and leap to his feet. His gill-like ears and long tapering face made him look like one of the fish that he was trying to catch. But he was lanky and round-shouldered, and not too old to run for his life. There was nobody else in sight.

Derek could get no answer out of him, and he rounded the mouth of the aqueduct and began stroking for shore. The instant the man realized what Derek was up to he turned and bolted the length of the aqueduct. Derek shot through the water like a fish.

The man himself did not appear to be armed. But he had to be kept from raising an alarm that might summon hordes of his own people down from the hills, armed and ready to kill. And what connection did he have with the Brotherhood of Diablo?

Although the man reached the shore well ahead of Derek, he did not seek the cover of the hills. Instead he sprinted straight down the open beach, as if confident that his speed alone would save him. And he was fast, very fast indeed. Derek dropped his sword and raced after him.

As the man sensed him gaining, he reverted to some very clever dodging techniques; and it took Derek nearly a quarter mile to run him down. He seemed less frightened than astonished that anybody could be so much faster and more agile than himself.

Derek hauled him back down the beach toward the aqueduct. "Now who are you?" he demanded. "Who lives here? Is this the land of the Brotherhood of Diablo?"

The man gaped at him, then vigorously shook his head. The shallow sea stretched north and south to the horizons; but far to the west, just above the turquoise blue waters, stood a chain of dark islands. The man pointed to the largest of these.

"Diablo," he said.

"Do you pay tribute to the Brotherhood of Diablo?"

Again the man vigorously shook his head.

"Then who rules the land around us?" asked Derek.

"The Wise Woman."

At that moment they saw Eva approaching them up the beach. She had retrieved the man's fishing pole; but it was Eva herself that seemed to astonish him the most. Gloriously naked, she was more splendid than any woman he had ever seen in his life. It took some time to get him settled down enough to tell his story. It was a very strange story. . . .

"It sounds like the contests of prowess in the *Iliad*," said Derek. "Do you remember when I read to you from that book?"

"Yes," said Eva. "The story of Helen of Troy. But I don't recall any such contests."

Derek turned back to the man. "Now what about this hobbling that you mentioned?"

"Those who lose in the contests, and those who displease Her Wisdom, are hobbled with weights. Thus they are surely captured by the Invincibles." Once more he pointed across the sea toward the looming island of Diablo. "They come when we least expect them, with ships and terrible dog-things. Once we could hide from them, but no longer. For no matter where we try to conceal ourselves, somehow they find us."

"And those who win the contests are allowed to live in peace?"

The man nodded. "I myself am registered for the dodge-and-dash contests." He glanced at Derek and sighed ruefully. But then he brightened. "Sometimes Her Wisdom does not hobble all the losers."

They watched him lope down the shingle with his fishing pole until he disappeared around a rocky headland, then turned and hurried back toward the aqueduct. Despite the man's promises and assurances, Derek wanted all his people safely out of the tunnel and into battle formation as soon as possible. He left his sword sticking in the sand.

The tide had turned, and they did not have to swim so far underwater this time. Soon the entire top of the vault was out of water. The men could now breathe air all the way to its mouth, and Derek rigged lines so that they could pull themselves along. He got an entire squadron of armed men out on the beach in good order.

But no enemy appeared. By late afternoon the tide had ebbed low enough for even the children to wade out of the aqueduct.

Derek chose a defensible hill about a mile inland, and Eva got everybody organized in preparing their camp for the night; everybody who wasn't fishing, that is. The man with the fishing pole had given Derek at least one good idea.

"Still nobody around," said Jana, as he returned to the beach.

She was seated by herself at the end of the aqueduct, gazing solemnly across the twilight-red waters of the sea. The islands to the west now stood on the horizon like the humps of a passing sea monster.

"He came to me just now," she said. "I wonder if he knows that I'm here, just across the sea?"

"Don't look so sad," he encouraged her. "Maybe you'll meet sooner than you think. Do you see that big dark island, the one that dominates all the rest? That's Diablo."

"I know," she said. "That's where he is."

*　　　*　　　*　　　*

A chain of hills screened the broad, rolling valley from the seashore. The valley stretched about two miles inland, and there were three passes into the foothills of the mountains, offering many possibilities for escape.

The Wise Woman's contests all seemed to be based on various methods of escaping pursuit: running, jumping, dodging, hiding, rock throwing; even the wrestling was really just an affair of breaking holds and getting away. There were seven events.

Derek had had more trouble than ever in deciphering his map; he was still not exactly sure where they were. What should have been the Central Valley of California was now the New Sea; and a distant chain of islands stood where his map indicated mountains. Nor was there much evidence of the vast population that had once dwelt here. The earth movements that had transformed this entire sector of the planet were almost beyond comprehension.

Nor did he yet understand why the so-called Wise Woman had needed so long to make a decision; weeks of haggling had passed without any form of agreement. Then all at once she had mysteriously scheduled the contests for this afternoon. Jana was especially troubled when she learned that the Wise Woman, for some unknown reason, had scheduled the hiding contest well before the others.

Thousands of people had already gathered at the convergence of the three passes that debouched into the valley. Most were young; all looked like fast runners.

Derek's own team was small but select: he himself was registered in the jumping and dodge-and-dash events, Gunnar in wrestling and rock throwing, Stinky in the distance run, and Jana in the hiding contest. Margo was not at all athletic; but she had insisted on coming along for reasons of her own.

Young Rollo had also wanted to come with them. He had been certain that he could hide at least as well as Jana, although he had never yet been able to sneak up on her unaware. But a brief demonstration had proven that he could neither hide from Jana nor discover her when she herself hid. Disgruntled, he had at last been forced to remain behind, determined to find out how she had rigged the demonstration.

Eva had remained behind with a better grace. She had turned out to be a surprisingly swift runner, but was not as swift as those already entered in the contests. She had assumed charge of the settlement until the others returned— victorious, of course; only then would they be allowed to dwell here in peace.

"Something's wrong," whispered Jana.

"They haven't moved since this morning, have they?" asked Derek.

She shook her head. The Brotherhood of Diablo had launched a slave raid somewhere up the coast; they were still there, about fifteen miles to the north. Jana had awakened Derek and Eva during the night, afraid that they themselves were being raided; but then the raiders had veered northwards.

"He's still with them," said Jana. "The one like me. Oh, I wish we didn't have these contests today!"

"We have to get them over with sometime," said Derek. "Is Buck where he's supposed to be?"

She was silent for a moment, then nodded. "But why do I have to go first? And where's this Wise Woman anyway? I'd like to get a peep at her."

"She's supposed to be here today. Maybe we'll finally get a chance to see her." He shrugged. "I really don't know why she scheduled the hiding contest so far before the others. Just do your best."

"I just hope Buck does his best. It would be very nice if he behaves himself for a change."

Her two opponents were wily little men in their early thirties; each was assigned one of the three passes out of the valley, each would have a separate band of trackers trying to find him. The band assigned to track Jana was the largest of all. Some of the men looked sheepish about tracking a little girl, and there were hoots of derision from the crowd, but the leaders appeared strangely determined, even relentless.

Jana herself was in no danger—so long as her trackers abided by the rules of the contest. Derek had taken precautions against any kind of treachery. The local people may have been capable of deadly harassment, but they were woefully ineffectual on the battlefield. He had let the Wise Woman know that she might find life precarious for a while, if she tried any tricks. And she had let him know that settled life here would be impossible under continual harassment by her people. Today's contest would determine whether their present accommodation would last.

"Teach 'em a lesson, small stuff!" cried Gunnar, as Jana took her place at the starting line.

She smiled and waved; although she still seemed troubled about something. Then a man stepped forward and waved a big yellow flag. There were shouts, applause, and more hoots of derision as the three contestants headed for their respective passes.

Few noticed the lone figure watching from a hilltop near the sea; he, too, had a big yellow flag. But nobody saw him wave it. He disappeared down the far side of the hill the instant the hiding contest began.

Jana's two opponents were out of sight before she even left the contest grounds. She had hardly entered the pass when her trackers came racing after her. But there was Buck, waiting faithfully in the shadows of an overhanging rock. She clambered onto his back, and they were gone.

Most of the trackers were dismayed to find the pass deserted; nor was there any sign of the little girl in the hills just beyond. Perhaps finding her would not be so simple after all.

Their leaders were more than just dismayed; they were horrified. They set out to capture Jana as if their very lives depended on it.

She was already well out of range on Buck's back, loping along toward a group of densely forested hills. Then he bounded up a slope that would discourage any human climbers, and they settled themselves comfortably in the shade. Buck still did not seem to open his eyes, although the deep shadows of the trees were obviously more to his liking.

Jana could see her pursuers a couple of miles away, poking futilely into every bush and coppice; at the rate they were moving it would take them hours just to reach the base of this hill—which they could hardly climb anyway. She put her hands behind her head, leaned comfortably back against a tree, and watched them with an impudent look on her face.

After a while, however, she realized what had been troubling her. She had been puzzled about the slave raid of the Brotherhood of Diablo even last night, although she had had no trouble following their movements down the northern coast, especially since the one like herself was with them. They had not moved since then—and that was what had been troubling her. Slave raiders would fan out over the countryside, not just sit in one place, as if they had never even left their ships. She tilted her little head to one side.

The next instant she was on her feet, peering frantically down through the trees. The trackers were not much closer, but they had fanned out over the countryside, the whole countryside. She had not realized that there were so many of them. Had they been secretly reinforced by trackers from the other bands? In any case, she could see no way of getting past them.

"Oh, Buck!" she cried. "What are we going to do?"

The litter scuttled swiftly toward the contest field. There were twelve bearers at each end, trained to run in step; the crowd scattered before them as if afraid of being trampled underfoot. The bearers very gingerly set the litter down where it could best command the entire vista, and sat meekly beside their poles. Then the curtain was yanked aside.

The Wise Woman was over a hundred years old; although hunched and shriveled, her presence was indeed formidable. Her face was painted in bizarre colors that made her look like some strange bird of prey; her raptorial eyes glittered with cunning and watchfulness. She surveyed the silent, deferential crowd as if challenging anyone even to question her absolute authority.

Then she started. A gaunt little girl was standing only a few feet away, staring at her with the avidity of a hungry cat-thing. She scowled but Margo only watched her more closely.

A score of wretched men and women came shuffling around the litter; they were hobbled with thongs; their ankles were tethered to heavy stone weights, which they were forced to lug wherever they went. They set the stones down with relief, and crouched obsequiously behind the litter.

The Wise Woman smiled with satisfaction. But when she turned back again she found the gaunt little girl still watching her avidly. Disconcerted, she made an impatient gesture for the contests to begin, and pretended to fall asleep. Only the keenest of eyes could have noticed the corner of one eyelid raise ever so slightly, then close again when she discovered that she was still being watched.

Margo at last moved away and began interrogating the hobbled men and women. They withheld nothing; evidently the Wise Woman was feared rather than loved, or even respected.

Derek had planned to enter the first event himself, but it turned out that points were awarded disproportionately to the heaviest stone cast, rather than the most accurate. Gunnar doffed his leather tunic to free his hocklike arms for the throw. His massive chest and shoulders were matted with black hair, and he stepped up to the line like a determined bear-thing. There were seventeen other contestants, including six women, and they watched him apprehensively.

The targets were striped pillows placed at varying distances along the course. Gunnar weighed the heaviest stone set out by the judges, then dropped it, shaking his head. The judges were amazed when he explained the problem to them. Only the Wise Woman herself could grant such a request.

She glared malevolently through the window of her litter, but Gunnar only grinned sheepishly back at her. She made an impatient gesture of assent and turned away, only to discover Margo watching her once more with cold calculation.

One of the hobbled men was then led forward and the stone tethered to his ankle cut loose. Gunnar hefted it with one hand, and returned to the line flipping it up and down like an apple. His toss landed with a heavy thud, just catching the edge of the third pillow. There were gasps from all sides, and the other seventeen contestants stealthily laid their own stones on the ground and faded into the crowd, trying to look inconspicuous. But the Wise Woman's eyes marked every one of them.

She herself had to select two men to oppose Gunnar in the wrestling contest, since none of the registered contestants could now be found. The object was to break the hold of a pursuer trying to make a capture. Once more Gunnar requested a change in the rules.

"We can end this business right now," he said. "Come on, lads, both of you at once."

He was awarded first hold; but though both men went almost berserk trying to break loose, they might just as well have been hobbled with weights. Then they tried to hold Gunnar—and found themselves shrugged off like a pair of kittens, landing hard on the ground several feet away. He grinned as the judges presented him with two strings of victory beads.

Derek turned out to be their least favored contestant. He won the jumping contest by a fair margin, but there were much faster runners here than the fisherman that he had run down on the beach. It was more his agility than his speed that brought him narrow victories in the two dodge-and-dash events.

The distance-run was the last contest, and the one that traditionally carried the most prestige. The Wise Woman was keenly interested. Stinky was built like her own fleet, long-legged people, and she had him summoned to her litter.

"It has been told me that you outrun the very animals of the mountains," she said in a harsh, croaking voice. "That you chase them toward the tall golden one, who is reputed to be a mighty hunter. Is this true? Speak!"

He nodded his little round head bashfully, looking everywhere but at her. "Sometimes, though, the c-critters won't be chased, and they chase m-me instead. Which ain't no f-f-fun at all.''

She glared at him, as if she suspected impudence. "They say that you could catch even the fleetest animals by yourself.''

"Probably c-could," he said thoughtfully. "Though I can't see how it'd d-do me much good to c-catch 'em. They'd just b-b-bite me and run off again.''

She waved him away disgustedly, and the judges led him back to the starting line. The course ran straight to the hills overlooking the seashore and back again, a distance of about three miles. But Stinky had trouble understanding the rules.

"Just watch what the others do," the judge said in exasperation.

"Can't very w-well do that," said Stinky. "Won't be n-nobody in front of me to watch." He frowned and closed one eye in concentration. "I just pick one of the flags off the p-p-pole by the beach and b-bring it back to prove I was there? Yeah, that ain't so h-hard.''

There were over a hundred men and women entered in this most prestigious of all events, and for the first hundred yards Stinky was busy just working his way to the front of the pack. Then he seemed to be the only one still moving. By the time the others had even begun to stretch out he was out of sight.

Meanwhile the two men in the hiding contest had been tracked down. The Wise Woman had them hobbled; but there was still no sign of Jana.

"After her!" she shrieked. "All of you!"

Jana had already won the contest. Further pursuit, especially this kind of mass pursuit, was clearly against the rules. There were some murmurs in the crowd. But as Derek hurried toward the Wise Woman's litter to protest, the crowd suddenly began to seethe about him. He never got even close.

The bearers snatched up the litter and vanished through the nearest pass like a frantic centipede. The hobbled men and women picked up their stone weights and shuffled pathetically in the same direction, but they were left far behind. Any pursuers would capture them instead of the Wise Woman.

For a few moments Derek, Gunnar, and little Margo were alone on the field. Then Stinky came racing toward them from one direction and Buck from the other.

"They're coming! They're coming!" cried Jana. "I tried, but I couldn't get back until all the trackers started to run and hide."

"Dog-things," cried Stinky. "Right b-behind me. Already caught some f-folks by the shore."

"Oh, Derek!" Jana cried. "The slave raiders are heading for our settlement. Eva will be trapped!"

Chapter 14: A Conversation With Willie

"Through interrogation of the Wise Woman's obsequious thralls—"

"Save your breath, kid," said Gunnar, glancing anxiously over his shoulder. "We got some running to do."

Margo did not reply. The pass through which the Wise Woman's litter had disappeared lay just ahead. There were hiding places there, and places where Derek and Gunnar might turn and make a stand.

"Looks like them big dog-things are rounding up people, not attacking 'em," said Gunnar. "They'll be after us soon."

They overtook the hobbled men and women, who were already exhausted from lugging their stone weights. The first pack of dog-things sent after the Wise Woman's litter would round them up, and they knew it. Derek ordered them to halt and drew his sword.

They cringed apprehensively; the Wise Woman prohibited weapons of any kind among her subjects, especially weapons that might be used for assassination. Derek quickly freed them from their hobbles and stone weights, but it was now too late to flee the dog-things charging straight at them across the valley.

"Stinky, take care of Margo," cried Derek. "We'll catch up with you later."

Gunnar had already lifted Jana onto a boulder, safely out of reach of the three dog-things rushing toward them across the valley. The beasts had been bred and trained specifically to hunt down human beings, and they had never yet been resisted. Neither had their masters, who could now be seen coming over the seaward hills. They, too, considered all humanity their lawful prey.

With their lips drawn back from savage fangs, the dog-things gave the impression of laughing viciously as they charged. Each stood nearly three feet high at the shoulder, and weighed a good hundred and fifty pounds.

But this was hardly a third of Buck's weight, and he did not consider himself the lawful prey of anything on earth. He crouched in the shadows of a volcanic outcrop near the mouth of the pass.

Bellowing and slavering with excitement, the three dog-things raced straight at their human quarry, as they had many times over the years. Buck hit them in the flank like an avalanche; the leader was killed instantly, its head nearly torn off. The other two were knocked sprawling. Buck pounced on them before they could even scramble back to their feet.

"I still don't know how he can see," Jana said, as Gunnar lifted her down from the boulder. "He never seems to open his eyes."

"What about the settlement?" asked Derek. "How close are they to it now?"

"Maybe two miles, or a little less. Oh, Derek!" she cried, standing on her tiptoes and peering toward the sea. "He's here, the one like me."

But Derek was only thinking about Eva and the rest of their people at the settlement. It was a good seven miles away, straight across the valley, which now teemed with the slave raiders and their packs of dog-things. The only safe route was through the hills, which meant at least twice the distance. Stinky was their best chance to send a warning.

"He's gone," said Jana, after a moment. "Looks like Margo decided just to keep going, and took Stinky with her. They seem to be moving in the direction of the Wise Woman."

"Well, you'll have to move in the direction of the settlement," said Derek. "Although that's a long run for Buck."

"He'd never make it back," said Jana. "How could I tell you what happened, even if I got there in time?"

Derek frowned; he didn't see any way in which a message. . . . "James Fenimore Cooper!" he cried, snapping his fingers. He quickly explained to Jana the principles of sending smoke signals. "If our people are safe, send up a whole lot of puffs. Otherwise, just send up three or four—then put out the fire.''

Buck sat calmly licking his paws amidst his slaughtered enemies; he had enjoyed the fight, and seemed more inclined to wait here in hopes that some more dog-things would attack than to do any running. But he sensed the urgency in Derek's voice, and bounded to his feet so that Jana could clamber onto his back.

"Eva, Buck! Eva!" she cried, and the great beast tore straight across the valley. The packs of dog-things were reluctant to pursue him, despite the angry commands of the slave raiders.

"Watch out, Derek!" cried Gunnar from behind. "We got company."

Derek whirled around and drew his sword, but the people who had entered the pass from behind did not seem at all hostile. He recognized some of them as runners who had competed in the contests. They all looked extraordinarily swift. A tall yellowish man with pendulous ear lobes stepped forward.

"My name is Peer. The wise little girl sent us to guide you."

"Margo? Where is she now?"

"She goes forth to challenge the Wise Woman." The murmurs all around left no doubt who these people hoped would win the contest—or, at least, who they hoped would lose. "But it is a dangerous thing for her. Only the Wise Woman knows the Sacred Books of Wisdom."

"We'll have to see about that later," said Derek. "Right now I need some place of vantage. A signal will soon come and I must be in a position to see it."

Peer nodded, and shouted to the others. Then they were moving again, out of the pass and into the hill country beyond. These were the fastest runners in a land of fast runners, and Derek knew that he would be hard pressed to keep up with them. Gunnar had no chance at all.

"It's no use," cried a lanky young woman, who had fallen back with Gunnar to see if she could improve his running style. "He does everything right. He is just slow."

"Then we must divide," cried Peer. "Lana, you and these others guide the slow one to a place of safety. We will lead Derek the Hunter to Losgatos Hill."

The landscape became increasingly rugged as they ran south, a ruggedness stressed everywhere by the shadows of the descending sun. It was a country of flinty hills and gulches, deeply scarred by the upheavals of a recent cataclysm.

"You should have no trouble hiding in country like this," said Derek, as they loped steadily along. "Even from a pack of dog-things."

"Once this was true," said his guide. "But now the Invincibles can find us no matter where we hide. Some suspect treachery." He did not name anyone, but added in a whisper: "Many hope that the wise little girl will succeed in her challenge."

As soon as Jana was sure that they were not pursued, she eased Buck into a steady lope. They had a long way to go, and he was more a creature of sudden bursts of power than endurance. The smoother gait also allowed her to see what was happening around her.

Several grotesque, hulking forms stood silhouetted on

the hills near the seashore; none weighed less than three hundred pounds, and they moved with the careless swagger of masters used only to obedience. It was late afternoon and the shadows groped across the valley like reaching arms. There was a dark line on the horizon to the southwest.

"Be careful," a voice suddenly whispered out of nowhere. "There are scouts just ahead of you."

Jana was so startled that she nearly tumbled headlong from Buck's back. For a moment her head swam and her heart fluttered with excitement. They could actually talk!

A tug at Buck's ear, and he dived into an erosion gulley and stopped. She quickly slipped from his back, sat down, and concentrated as she had never concentrated in her life.

"The people you're hunting have been good to me," she thought. "Can you help them?"

After a long silence: "I've stopped the hunt for a few minutes. That's really all I can do now, although it may help some of your friends to escape. They're just over the next ridge from us. Can you find them?"

"Yes, they seem to be moving away from our settlement. Every minute counts, so the longer you delay them—" She felt the sudden stab of pain. "Oh, was it bad?"

"They stick me with needles whenever they think I'm playing tricks on them. Which I always do whenever I get the chance. But it's getting dark, and the Rathugs are impatient."

"Rathugs?"

"That's what most people call them, including me. Not to their faces, of course. They call themselves the Invincibles or the Brotherhood of Diablo. The first part of the name comes from their big fortress, the Rath of Diablo. I don't know if the second part comes from *thugs* or *ugly*—either one applies.''

The scouts had moved, and now only a hundred yards of open country separated them. Jana did not want to bring Buck any closer—he enjoyed fighting too much, no matter how badly outnumbered.

''Stay, Buck! Stay!'' she whispered, and crept out of the erosion gulley.

''Are you running?'' came the voice.

''Yes, but I'm not very fast.''

''Neither am I. That's why they always catch me whenever I run away. And it's hard to hide from their nasty dog-things, so be very careful.''

The Invincibles were just on the other side of the knoll. Jana crept forward on her hands and knees and peeked over the top. Rathugs, dog-things, and swarms of slaves milled impatiently about in the shadows below. There were several wheeled cages—fortunately still empty. A hulking monstrosity with a humped back, his body covered with tufts of reddish-brown hair, screened her view; he held a chain in his hand, but she could not see what was attached to its other end.

''My people have almost escaped,'' she said. ''Can you delay them just a little longer?''

''I'll try, although they never really believe anything I say. But they're worried that I might be sick, because I started to tremble when I felt you getting close. That's how I got them to stop. If anything happens to me, they'll have to answer to the Rathagon himself, and he's the nastiest of them all. By the way, my name is Willie, they think I'm some kind of little boy.''

"My name is Jana. My people think I'm some kind of little girl."

"Then it seems we're suited to each other."

Jana started to laugh but she was stopped by another sudden stab of pain. "Willie, are you all right?"

"Now I've done it. I burst out laughing, and now they're all sure that I was playing a trick on them."

"Will they punish you?"

"They'll probably make me stand on my knees all day, or keep me awake all night. But I'm always catching it for something or other. I wish your friends were a little farther away."

So did Jana. Men shouted and cursed, whips cracked, dog-things whined excitedly and pulled at their leashes: the hunt had resumed. But now she could see Willie, sitting on a rock with a chain around his neck; he had his back turned, but he had the same red-golden hair that she did and was exactly the same size.

"Watch out!" he warned her.

Jana instantly turned and scrambled back down the slope. In her excitement she had forgotten to keep her defenses up, and one of the scouts had come up behind her. Had he seen her? She ran and ran, until her little legs felt heavy and she gasped for breath. Then there was a shout, and the whole troop of slave raiders seemed to be descending on her. Dog-things howled in pursuit.

At that moment a lithe, naked figure appeared on the ridge directly above. It was Eva! She raced across the very summit of the ridge, in full view of the raiders, almost as if she wanted them to see her. They had never seen a woman so beautiful. The hunt now concentrated on her alone.

But one scout had come up behind Jana. She lost sight of Eva as she dived through the thorny underbrush, but the man was right behind her, gaining with every stride. Not even Buck's keen ears could have picked up her cries for help at such a distance. She wished now that she had not ordered him to stay.

The scout's footsteps pounded behind her, and she tried futilely to dodge back and forth. Then all at once there was a tremendous thud—and silence.

When she looked back she saw Buck licking his paws beside the torn carcass of the scout. He had disobeyed her again—and for once she was glad.

Now she had to get him out of sight. There were twenty big dog-things after Eva, and Buck was sure to attack the moment he saw them, no matter what orders she gave him. He would only be dragged down at last, and it would not save Eva from capture.

Then she almost cried out. Eva had already been captured; she was now somewhere on the other side of the ridge, surrounded by the entire troop of slave raiders.

"What happened?" Willie's voice broke in. "And what in the world is that with you? The same beast-thing you were with when we first came close enough to talk?"

"Yes, he saved me from the scout. His name is Buck, the beast-thing of Derek the Hunter."

"That's the name! Derek the Hunter! They don't usually send me on routine slave raids, but this time they were after somebody special. I overheard them talking just before we sailed from Diablo. They thought if they attacked the settlement here, that this Derek the Hunter would come to its defense and then they could capture him.''

"He would have come, except that he sent me instead. I'm supposed to send a message. But why is your voice getting so weak?''

"We're moving fast—back to the ships.''

"Then the hunt is over?''

"They've had to call it off. Can you see those dark clouds moving in from the southwest? Well, the ships of the Brotherhood of Diablo are kind of slow and clumsy, and they're not very good sailors. They think a storm is coming, and they're afraid of being blown off course and separated. The Fisherfolk sometimes attack single ships that drift too far north.''

"They won't punish you for their failure, will they?''

"Nothing worse than usual. They need me for some big invasion that they're planning. Besides, they've captured a very great prize—the most beautiful woman I've ever seen.''

"Her name is Eva. She is the woman of Derek the Hunter. Will they hurt her?''

"They've put a collar around her neck, and a Rathug is leading her by a chain. But she's too great a prize for them to touch. The Rathagon himself will make the judgment.'' His voice was getting weaker and weaker. "There'll be feasting and revelry for many days and nights before they send her inland to the Rath of Diablo. They keep me in a cage and make me watch. It's so awful!''

Jana could feel his shudder of loathing and disgust. "Can you help Eva? She sacrificed herself so that the others could escape.''

"Yes, I know. She's very brave, and if. . . . The moon will be nearly full. . . . Don't. . . ." And then nothing.

Evidently they could only talk when they came within about two miles of each other. But now Jana was faced with another terrible decision. Which signal should she send Derek? He would surely die if he tried to rescue Eva now—and he would. And Eva would still be carried away to a place of evil. Perhaps it was better to send no signal at all. Willie would help them rescue Eva, if they could somehow find a ship to Diablo. . . .

She rode Buck to the top of a hill, where she could overlook the valley and the seashore beyond. The hulking galleys of the Brotherhood of Diablo were being dragged back into the water; at this distance the swarms of slaves looked like ants around a line of fat black caterpillars. The two ships they left on the beach were of different sizes; the larger apparently awaited the raiders returning from the settlement, the smaller transported the dog-things and their handlers. The New Sea was still aflame with the twilight sun, but dark clouds were now rolling in from the southwest.

Jana watched helplessly as the troop with Eva and Willie emerged from behind a ridge and turned toward the beach. Then she became aware of Buck whining. He had turned his face away from the sun, and now she turned that way too. There was no need for messages any more.

"Derek, Buck!" she cried. "Derek!"

The great beast had had a long day of running and fighting, but he had recognized his master scrambling down into the valley, even miles away. Derek had evidently seen Eva being led toward the slave ships. Jana hoped desperately that he would not reach them in time, for then his own death would be certain. There was no holding Buck as he raced toward Derek.

She could not bear to stand and watch, so she turned and began what seemed like the longest journey of her life. It was after dark when she finally reached their deserted settlement. A log cabin was the first structure that she came to, and she lay down and sobbed herself to sleep.

CHAPTER 15: THE LAST SHIP TO DIABLO

Most of the wheeled cages returned to the ships empty; so costly an expedition was hardly justified by the returns, as far as Derek could see. But there was still no signal from Jana, and he began to fear that she herself had been captured by the slave raiders. And Eva? He scanned the ridges to the south for signs of smoke.

The men around him on the hilltop relaxed as they saw the hulking galleys being heaved back into the water. Only two were now left on the beach; strings of dog-things were being coaxed up a ramp into the smaller of them. Dark clouds rolled in out of the southwest, and there was talk of a storm. But Derek was only interested in the southern skies, and he watched more and more anxiously for Jana's signal.

Then he felt a tug at his arm. Peer lay beside him on the ledge overlooking the valley, and he directed Derek's attention toward a procession just emerging from behind a ridge near the seashore. It marched rapidly toward the larger of the two remaining ships.

"The last of the Invincibles. They fear a storm and hurry to put to sea. Rejoice that we are not their galley slaves, for they will be hard driven until the ships are safely past the Great Channel. Ah," he cried with relief, "those last cages are empty."

Derek was even more relieved. The wheeled cages were returning empty from the direction of his own settlement. A threatening storm had saved his people this time, and there would be no next time. Never again would he leave them so exposed to danger, no matter what assurances he was given by the Wise Woman. But why hadn't Jana signaled? He glanced once more toward the southern skies; then back again.

Then he was on his feet, staring in horror. At the very end of the procession, led by a chain around its neck, strode a proud, erect figure that was unmistakable. He ignored the cries of alarm behind him as he vaulted from the ledge. Leaping, running, sliding, he reached the valley floor within seconds.

Even his great speed was not enough; the distance was too far. He had to pace himself or he would reach the ship too exhausted to fight. But what could he do against so many? He dismissed the question from his mind. Eva's life and his own had become identical, and he ran on with what seemed like maddening slowness.

Even more maddening was the fact that he could no longer see the ships, or even the procession approaching them. The chain of hills screening the seashore glowed like living coals in the rays of the setting sun. Then all at once they were extinguished. The dark rolling blanket of clouds swept across the horizon. His lungs burned and his driving legs grew heavy, but he never slackened the fastest pace that he dared.

Gritting his teeth with the effort, he charged up the hillside and at last gazed down at the beach. He was too late! The ship carrying Eva had already put to sea, and its banks of oars rhythmically carried her farther and farther away from him. The waters of the New Sea were now a dull, metallic gray, and in his frenzy he even thought of plunging into them and swimming after the ship until his strength failed and he drowned.

But there was still another galley on the beach, a smaller vessel. Perhaps he could capture it, use it somehow to follow Eva into the very heart of Diablo itself.

The sand was still hot from the burning afternoon sun; its dryness made running difficult. It was growing dark now, and the onshore breeze kept the last strings of dog-things still on the beach from scenting him.

Slaves gathered about the hull of the clumsy ship, ready to launch it the moment the order was given. There was only one Invincible still on shore, and he turned and ordered the handlers to untie the remaining dog-things from their pegs and get them aboard.

It was at that instant that he spotted Derek charging

across the sand. At first he was only surprised; it took several moments for him to realize that somebody was actually daring to attack him. He was a hulking, beetle-browed monstrosity, weighing well over three hundred pounds, but he was also a trained warrior. He drew his sword and assumed a defensive posture with surprising quickness for anyone so huge. It was his misfortune to be hit with something for which not even a lifetime of military drilling had prepared him, something almost never met with in human combat—total attack.

The ship taking Eva away was still in sight, and the last remaining ship was even now being launched; whips cracked, orders were bellowed, dog-things snarled and howled and tugged wildly at their leashes. But Derek could do nothing to stop the launching until he got past the monstrosity facing him. He attacked with a frenzy and desperation that made him at that instant perhaps the most savage fighter on the face of the planet.

But so hulking a creature took a lot of killing. By the time Derek had slain him the ship was already in the water; Derek vaulted over the body as it collapsed onto the sand, and raced in pursuit.

Most of the slaves had already scrambled aboard, but there was still two strings of dog-things left on shore, tearing at their leashes and snarling wildly in their futile attempt to reach Derek. Screams of rage from the deck became orders for them to be loosed. But the handlers were too stunned by the sight of the hulking corpse to obey. An Invincible had been killed!

Then Buck was among the dog-things, and total attack was the only way he ever fought; the noise and fury were like a natural cataclysm. The handlers ran futilely back and forth as if the whole world was coming to an end.

Derek plunged into the sea after the retreating ship, and for a few yards actually gained on it. But then the resistance of the water slowed him to a halt, and he could only stand waist deep, trembling with anger and frustration, and watch helplessly as the galley pulled slowly away from him.

But the ship hove to about fifty yards off shore. In the deepening twilight Derek could just make out the brutish, hulking form standing amidships. The racket on the beach behind him did not quite drown the voice that now bellowed across the water.

"I know who you are, Derek the Hunter. The Rathagon himself has decreed your death, and soon we will come back for you."

"Herder of dog-things," cried Derek. "Terror of the weak and sick, I have now killed two of the Brotherhood of Diablo. Come and be the third! Do you cower before my challenge? Do you fear that your slaves will learn that you are not really invincible? Come back and I will prove it to them!"

But there was no reply. The crack of a whip sounded across the water, followed by the rhythmic plash of oars, and the galley pulled away slowly into the dusk. The ship carrying Eva was already out of sight.

With an effort of will Derek tried to master himself. Anger and frustration would not rescue Eva; only cold, clear thinking. Somehow he had to find a ship to go after her—and soon. The one thing he tried not to think about was what might happen to her on Diablo.

There were five handlers left behind on shore, cowering near their slaughtered dog-things. Beaten, starved, their spirits crushed by slavery, they were a sorry lot of human vermin. Four lay grovelling on their bellies, whining and pleading; the fifth was an emaciated old man, who at least stood on his own feet. He watched Derek suspiciously, but he neither begged nor tried to run away.

"What is your name?" asked Derek. "And where do you come from?"

The man was not as old as he had looked. Ragged, unwashed, his ribs protruding like slats across his wasted chest; he was probably not over forty, although his hair was prematurely white. Brown-gray blotches covered his body and there was something strange about the shape of his mouth; but his spirit had somehow survived.

"I am called Korso, and I come from the land of the Fisherfolk, to the north." His voice was husky, as if he had grown unaccustomed to speaking. "Many years ago the Brotherhood of Diablo captured our ship. I am the only one still alive." He noticed Derek staring at his shoulder, and turned so that he could see what survival had cost him. His back was a livid sheet of scar tissue. "The whips of the Brotherhood of Diablo are not for their dog-things alone."

"Couldn't you have escaped?"

"Three times have I escaped. But I was always recaptured and given over to be tormented. Only when I begged them for death did they let me live. None can escape them, for they are cunning and merciless. Were I not useful to them as a handler, they would have sent me to the butchery long ago." He nodded contemptuously at the men grovelling in the sand. "This is what usually becomes of those useful to the Brotherhood of Diablo. Their souls have been crushed, their minds left hardly superior to the dog-things that they handle."

"Then you know the ways of Diablo," said Derek. "How may I get there as soon as possible?"

The man looked curiously at him. "I saw you kill one Invincible, and another slink from your challenge. And I heard him call your name. Until now I did not really believe that such a person as Derek the Hunter really existed. Even in the dungeons beneath the Rath of Diablo your name is whispered—"

"Just tell me how I may reach Diablo quickly. Nothing matters now but that."

"By ship is the only way."

"What of your people, the Fisherfolk? Can I get such a ship from them?"

"You said that you wanted to reach Diablo quickly. It would take you weeks to reach the northern realm of the Fisherfolk."

"Then where may I get a ship? Never mind how dangerous or difficult it might be."

Korso nodded, "I understand. The woman captured by the last hunting party was special to you? God help her if they know this." He coughed and swallowed, then continued in a weak, raspy voice. "Be patient, it is many years since I've talked so much. The only way of getting a ship quickly is from the Brotherhood of Diablo itself. One of them has been killed, and slaves left behind. They will send a scout ship to spy out the land."

"When?"

"Late tomorrow, at the earliest. But my guess is the day after." He added doubtfully, "You may be able to capture the ship."

"I will capture it, no matter what." He hesitated before asking, as if afraid of the answer: "What will they do with the woman? Tell me, even if it is very bad."

"She is a great prize, more beautiful than any woman I have ever seen. She will be judged by the Rathagon himself."

Derek felt his shoulders slumping in despair. "Then she will be sent into this Rath of Diablo?"

"Yes, but probably not right away. The raiders will first spend some days and nights in feasting and revelry, in the butchery and torment of captives. Only then will they send their prizes inland to the Rath."

"Send? The raiders themselves will not march inland?"

He replied sadly, "A great fleet is now gathering in Colinga Harbor to attack my people, to punish them because they are still free. It is rumored that strange machines are also being gathered—for what use, I don't know. The Rathagon has declared the total subjection of all peoples who still refuse him tribute. But the raiders that came here today will not want to share their booty with others, so they will first hold their revel in a secret place. Probably near the sea."

Derek started to reply, but a low growl from Buck caused him to turn around. Several dark shapes crept warily toward them out of the hills.

"It's Peer," cried the tall yellowish man out of the darkness. "Don't let your dog-thing attack us. We come to help you."

216

As Derek restrained Buck, the slaves on the sand began to moan in terror. Even Korso looked apprehensive.

"They will kill us all," he whispered. "For we have helped the Brotherhood of Diablo to hunt them."

"There will be no more killing tonight!" Derek cried decisively.

After a moment's hesitation, he heard the thud of large stones as they were dropped to the ground. Then the men approached once more, but not too close to Buck. Lightning bolts shot from the sky like the legs of some monstrous insect stalking them out of the southwest; the sea looked oily and the air was oppressively still.

"You say that you've come to help?" said Derek. "Then prove it." He already had made a rough plan for the capture of the scout ship; but he could not accomplish it alone. "A ship from the Brotherhood of Diablo will come here tomorrow or the next day. I plan to capture it."

The men gasped at such audacity; but they were suspicious of Korso, and would not reply until he had moved out of earshot.

"We dare not help you without the consent of the Wise Woman," said Peer, and the others nodded.

"I understand," said Derek. "But all I really want is her promise not to interfere. My own people will give me all the help I need." The surprise vital to his plan for capturing the scout ship could be destroyed by even ineffectual harassment from the people of the Wise Woman.

Peer glanced down the beach toward Korso and whispered, "We will carry your message to the Wise Woman, and then return to help you. Many of us think we should fight back and not always run away. But the Wise Woman has ruled us time out of mind. . . .'' He shrugged.

He did not have to say any more; Derek knew the fate of all those who displeased the Wise Woman. But he still did not know what had become of either Jana or Gunnar.

Peer said, ''The bearded slow one is being cared for by Lana.'' He added with a hint of amusement, ''Very well cared for, in fact. But depend on us, Derek the Hunter. We will bring you the Wise Woman's decision by morning.''

''Good. I'll wait for you at our settlement. And one more thing.'' He glanced up at the darkening sky. ''The storm may not come this far north, but I'd like you to get these men to shelter. Can I depend on you not to harm them?''

They agreed reluctantly and prodded the whimpering slaves to their feet and led them back toward the hills. Korso alone remained behind.

He said dryly, ''Can I depend on your dog-thing not to harm me?''

''We have a long walk,'' said Derek. ''Let's talk on the way. Come on, Buck! Storm or no storm, we have to keep moving.''

He was anxious to find out what had happened to Jana; it seemed that all the rest of his people had somehow evaded the slave raiders. He was also anxious to learn all he could about the island of Diablo. Two green lights followed them through the starless night.

CHAPTER 16: WATCHING THE HORIZON

Jana yawned and stretched. There had been a storm during the night, and the log cabin was dank and chilly, smelling of stale food and bedclothes and cold ashes. She pulled the quilt around her thin little body and shivered. It was just dawn.

The settlement had remained deserted until just a few hours ago. It was Buck who had found her here; but Derek had let her go back to sleep, once he knew that she was safe. He had brought a strange man with him, and now they were all asleep in Derek's tent.

Then she realized that there was somebody else prowling about the settlement. What was young Rollo doing here so early? Gritting her teeth, she at last hopped out of her nice warm bed and looked around for something to eat. The nutbread was not very fresh, but it was not exactly stale either, and she ate two big slices, washed down with a mug of cold herb tea.

After scrubbing her little face and hands until they were rosy, she slipped out the door. The morning sun was obscured by a bank of dark clouds far to the east, and the ground was still damp and soggy from last night's storm. She flitted through the gloom like a shadow.

Another log cabin near the edge of the settlement was still under construction, and she crept forward and peeked around the corner. Rollo had a knife in his hand; his eyes darted warily from side to side, and he stopped again and again to listen. She admired his courage, and wished that there were some way she could avoid hurting his feelings, but there was none. She stepped out into the open.

He was startled at first but then relaxed into a slow burn. He muttered something that Jana chose not to hear, spat, kicked a pebble, and shook his head in disgust.

"And just what are you doing here? Where's my father, and Derek and Eva?" He had come back on his own to explore the settlement, when many were afraid that the slave raiders might have set a trap. And here was this simpering little nuisance again! "Oh, what do you know about anything!"

"Derek guessed that it would be you," Jana said innocently.

"Guessed what?"

"That it would be Gunnar's son who would be the first

one to come back. He sent me with an important message for you.''

The boy nodded and slipped his knife complacently back into its scabbard. "What's the message?"

"Derek wants you to return to our people, and lead them back here to the settlement. The slave raiders have gone."

"Is my father here?"

"I think Derek said that he was with the local people, somewhere on the far side of the valley."

"Well, I didn't really expect you to know exactly. But you can tell Derek that I'll get the people back here soon. They're camped about a mile east of here."

Jana knew that they were really about two and a half miles away, in the foothills to the southeast. But she smiled admiringly at Rollo, and watched him turn and trot away. Then she headed for Derek's tent.

Buck was asleep, sprawled across the entrance. He awoke at her approach, wagged his tail drowsily, and fell asleep again. She had to crawl over him to get inside.

Derek slept on his own quilted bed, which he normally shared with Eva. The stranger slept on a pallet nearby, and he turned restlessly in his sleep as Jana entered the tent. She winced at the sight of his scarred back and shoulders.

She was not a very good cook and prudently kept the breakfast menu as simple as possible. Lighting the fire, she whipped up some batter and set the table. The pancake flour had been ground from the seeds of certain wild grasses; by itself it had a rich nutty flavor. But the eggs were from a kind of gull and always made the pancakes taste fishy. Buck was standing beside her as she started to fry the meat, and she had to give him some.

"Derek," she whispered. "It's breakfast time."

The touch of a cold nose against his back brought Derek suddenly to a sitting position. The stranger's reaction was even more dramatic. Prodded by a huge paw, he sleepily rolled over—and dived out the tent door, shrieking with fright. He returned a few moments later, wide awake and looking rather sheepish.

They were all hungry, and Jana told them about everything that had happened since she rode off to warn the settlement. Everything, that is, except Willie. That was for Derek's ears alone. He smiled at the tactful way in which she had gotten Rollo to bring the people back to the settlement.

"We'll need them," he said.

It was as Jana started to refill their mugs with herb tea that she realized that the stranger was watching her curiously.

"You're exactly the same!" he cried. "For just a moment I thought that you might actually. . . . But, no, the Brotherhood of Diablo would never lose anything so precious to them. They keep the poor little fellow on a chain."

Derek said, "I know about him. If he's kept anywhere near Eva, rescue may be . . . well, difficult."

"No, no," cried Jana. "He's my friend!"

Perhaps there was no need to be quite so secretive about Willie after all. But she was still reluctant to discuss the more intimate details of their encounter in front of the stranger. She caught Derek's eye.

"Looks like Buck is still hungry," he said. "Yesterday

was a long day for him. Korso, will you go and get another joint of meat? The larder is the log building straddling the brook.''

He looked from one to the other; then smiled grimly. ''I get it. Take your time, it will probably take me a while to get the meat.''

Derek had not been surprised that Eva would sacrifice herself to save the rest of the people. But he was astonished when he heard about Willie.

''You mean you can actually talk with him?''

''Only when we get within about two miles of each other. But he's promised to help Eva, although most of the time they keep him locked in a cage, and stick him with needles when he tricks them. I'm going to Diablo with you,'' she added firmly.

He was silent for a moment; then nodded. ''Yes, I'll have to take you with me. Korso told me a lot about Diablo on the way back here last night, but even he isn't sure where the raiders have taken Eva. It will probably be somewhere near the sea. I don't know what we can do if they take her inland to the Rath of Diablo before we get there.''

''I'll find her, Derek.'' She took his hand affectionately. ''No matter where they take her.''

''Did your friend Willie tell you about the Mogs?''

She shook her head. ''There wasn't time to talk about anything except Eva. But he said the same thing about where the slave raiders would take her. Although he called them Rathugs, not Mogs.''

''They're not the same thing. Korso told me that the Rathagon has a bodyguard of these Mogs, which really are invincible in battle. I saw some of them back at the aqueduct—with the hunting party. They're over nine feet tall.''

"We're taking Buck with us, aren't we?" said Jana. "In case we have to do some fast running."

"Yes, we'll have to take Buck. Although I don't know yet how we're going to get him on and off the ship—assuming the Wise Woman lets us capture one."

Jana said very quietly, "Maybe you could just let her know that it wouldn't be very wise to try and stop us."

"You sound like Margo now," he said, laughing. "I wonder what's become of her since she went after the Wise Woman, and took Stinky with her? I think she was up to something."

"When isn't she? But you can ask Stinky himself, in a few minutes. He's on his way here now."

Stinky was not even breathing hard when he finally arrived, although he had run all the way from the far side of the valley without stopping. He was sweating, however, and Jana opened the tent flaps and tied them back.

"Had your breakfast yet?" said Derek.

"Yes, b-but I can always eat another. Funny eggs they got around here, though. Taste like f-f-fish." He tucked in with a good appetite.

"Now what about Gunnar and Margo?" asked Derek.

He threw back his little round head and guffawed. "Doing r-real good, both of 'em." He grinned doggishly. "And little Margo's sharper than ever."

"Is she with the Wise Woman?"

"Never g-goes far away. Watching and asking sly questions and p-p-poking into everything. You know h-how she is. Looks to me like the Wise Woman's r-runnin' scared. Creepy old thing!''

"I'm waiting for a message from her.''

"Be here in a l-little while, I expect. Gang of 'em started this way b-before I did. I w-was going to ask what they was up to, b-b-but they all started racing the minute they saw me. 'Course then I h-had to show 'em what real running is all about.'' He guffawed. ''Bet they thought something h-had 'em by the leg.''

They arrived a few minutes later, and it was not long afterwards that the rest of Derek's people began to straggle wearily back into the settlement. The women were relieved to find their tents and cabins untouched; the men were ready to follow Derek anywhere. They knew that few of them would have escaped but for Eva.

Late that afternoon was the earliest they could expect a scout ship, and Derek was determined to be ready in good time. They would only get one chance, and if they failed. . . . He pushed the thought from his mind as he recruited his men and organized the settlement for defense. Gunnar would probably have done the job more efficiently—certainly Eva would have—but he managed to get it done well before noon.

The women helped to braid, splice, and coil down ropes; there were seventeen baskets of these by the time they were ready to march. But Derek was still not really confident of his plan for grappling the ship. What if it never came close enough to shore? Even Korso doubted that it would actually land.

A few pearlescent clouds drifted lazily out of the west. The sea was calm, and there was no sign of any bad weather that might delay the scout ship. Nor did it look like the Wise Woman would actively interfere.

"We can help you carry food, weapons, anything at all," said Peer. "Although Her Wisdom has forbidden any of our people to help you with the actual capture of the ship." He glanced around to see that they were not overheard. "Beware of treachery, Derek the Hunter," he whispered.

Prayers were said for the success of the venture. More and more people, especially the women, had begun to wear crucifixes; Mathew and the others rescued from the Children of Satan instructed and counseled them in matters of faith. It was Mathew himself who now led the prayers.

Peer and the men and women with him volunteered to lug the heaviest baskets. Nothing had changed on the beach since last night, although the dead Rathug and the carcasses of the dog-things slaughtered by Buck had been partially devoured. A dense flock of carrion birds still circled not far above, watching for a chance to return to their interrupted meal.

Another troupe of the Wise Woman's people arrived on the beach, escorting Gunnar. They too were under orders not to assist actively in the capture of the ship, but when they had talked with Peer's people, each encouraging the other, they resolved to stay and help anyway. This day would be commemorated long afterwards as the time when their people first began to fight back against the Brotherhood of Diablo.

Gunnar started growling orders the moment his feet touched the sand. The leader of the troupe that had escorted him looked very pleased with herself, and she sauntered over to the women who had come with Peer. They laughed and whispered among themselves. Gunnar did not seem to notice their glances. He did not come over to Derek and Jana until everything was arranged to his own satisfaction.

"Why are you tying rocks to the ends of those ropes?" he asked. He did not look down at Jana, although he was aware of the mischievous grin on her little face.

Derek said, "You've seen the bolas I hunt small game with. Same principle." He called the others around him. "A demonstration is probably the best way of explaining."

Selecting a nearby sapling as his target, he whirled the rope over his head like his bolas and let fly. He overcompensated for the greater weight of these stones and the attached length of rope, hitting the sapling higher than he had intended. But his aim was straight, and the stones spun round and round the upper branches. He pulled the rope taut, bending the sapling to the ground. Eager murmurs arose all about him.

Gunnar gnawed at his beard and wiped his big paw across his forehead. "I get it," he said at last. "When this ship comes close enough we pull it in like you did with that sapling? Here, let me try that a couple of times."

Then ropes were arcing through the air up and down the length of the beach. Rock throwing was an admired skill among the people of the Wise Woman, and they mastered the technique much more readily than Derek's own people. Unfortunately they were not very robust. If they did manage to snare the scout ship, they would need a lot of help in dragging it toward shore. Derek and Gunnar worked through most of the afternoon with the organization and drill.

Stinky had no objection to watching others work in the hot sun, and he found a nice shady spot in which to relax. Jana sat nearby with Buck, although she concentrated on other things than ropes flying through the air. Most of the time she sat with her little head tilted slightly to one side, as if listening to something very faint and far away. It was midafternoon when she at last rose and hurried over to Derek.

"They're coming," she said. "I can't tell yet how many—about fifty, I'd guess—but there are dog-things with them, lots of dog-things."

"The numbers sound high," said Korso. "They would not send so many on a mere scouting voyage, and scouts rarely take dog-things with them. But nobody has ever killed an Invincible before, so they may seek revenge."

"Perhaps they'll beach their ship after all," said Derek.

"Not until they are sure of a safe landing. First they will send a handler and a string of dog-things ashore in a rowboat." He added with satisfaction. "I would probably have been the one they sent—if they still had me."

Gunnar joined them. He had never mentioned Eva's capture to Derek, although he knew why they were here and why it was so important that they capture the scout ship. No words were necessary; nor could any be enough. At that moment two of the local women sauntered past him on their shapely runner's legs and smiled invitingly. Gunnar was very careful not to look down at Jana.

"Wish we could be sure that they'll come close enough to shore," he said. "If they do . . ." He nodded his head significantly. "We got all the men we need to make sure they never get away again."

"We're about to get some more men," said Jana. "Whether we need them or not. But we certainly don't need the Wise Woman right now. There's the ship."

Chapter 17: Margo Disposes

A black speck emerged over the horizon, growing rapidly in size as it surged toward them, across the turquoise blue waters of the New Sea. The scout ship was traveling at top speed, every square inch of its black sails spread before the wind, and the oars of its tormented galley slaves lashed the sea with an ominous rhythm. It seemed to fear nothing on Earth.

"Lucky the breeze is onshore," said Korso. "The dog-things won't pick up our scent and make their handlers suspicious."

"They'll be more than just suspicious if they see us here on the beach," said Derek.

"I'll handle that," said Gunnar. It took him only minutes to chase everybody out of sight behind the row of hills. Then he took up his own position out of sight.

Meanwhile the litter of the Wise Woman was moving directly toward the beach. Soon it would become visible even far out to sea.

"That's the last thing we need right now," Jana groaned. "She always seems to know exactly when we don't want her around. But at least Margo is still safe. She's on her way here now with Her Creepiness."

Derek quickly beckoned to Stinky. "Do you see the litter of the Wise Woman? Get to it as fast as you can, and tell her that she must stop at once. If anything makes the ship suspicious, all our chances of capturing it will be lost." He did not have to add that Eva would also be lost—forever.

Stinky seemed ready and willing to do any amount of running in the opposite direction from the approaching black scout ship.

"That what you m-mean?" he said. "Way across the v-valley there?"

Derek nodded. "Yes, try and keep the hills between yourself and the sea while you're running. I'll be right behind you."

Stinky grinned at this, but any remarks he might have made were silenced by the look in Derek's eyes. He took a deep breath, threw back his head, and shot through a gap in the hills like a dust devil.

For the first fifty yards or so Derek kept up, but Stinky soon pulled away. Derek could see the Wise Woman's litter about a mile ahead, surrounded by a large entourage. But Stinky was almost there. Would the Wise Woman stop, or simply ignore him and continue on, becoming ever more visible to the nearing ship?

Then he realized that he was no longer alone, that something was overtaking him. It was Buck, with little Jana clinging valiantly to his shaggy coat. Derek turned out to be the last one to reach the litter.

Fortunately it had already halted for Stinky, and stood safely concealed in the lee of a wooded hill. Its curtains were still drawn as usual, but the bearers lounged and sauntered about with unusual freedom, and a small perch had been built onto its rear. A huddled figure sat there like a footman, obscured by the body of the litter itself.

Then came a muffled command from inside, and the Wise Woman's chief attendant scurried forward and obsequiously held open the door. But it was not the Wise Woman herself who now emerged. It was Margo.

She seemed, even for her, unusually drawn and pale; there was a telltale redness about her eyes, as if she had returned to her old Saluston habit of reading all night. But there was nothing infirm or hesitant about her. If anything, her characteristic intensity appeared to have redoubled.

"I'm glad to find you safe, Margo," said Derek. "But Eva has been captured by the Brotherhood of Diablo, and I must speak with the Wise Woman."

"Then speak," said Margo complacently.

"That's her perched on the back of the litter," whispered Jana.

But Margo merely turned and clapped her hands three times. "You may repose inside whilst I confer with my friends, Clara."

The old woman crawled down from her perch, scuttled

obediently into the litter, and drew the curtain. Derek and Jana stared at each other in wonder.

Margo only looked at them more complacently than ever. "Your desired converse with the Wise Woman may now proceed. For I am she."

Derek might have laughed, had the scout ship not been so close, and its capture so vital. Margo already knew most of the things that he now told her, but she made some changes in his plan for capturing the ship, simplifying it and at the same time providing for any contingencies, thus making it more certain of success.

"You say that this ship won't be here for an hour yet?" said Margo. "Then let us perambulate. Since you now have an infallible plan for the sequestration of yon approaching vessel, there is neither urgency nor immediate peril. Shall I usefully employ the time at our disposal in a recapitulation of the events actuating my assumption of suzerainty over the lands and perquisites of the quondam Wise Woman?"

"If you think you can do it in an hour," Jana said dryly.

But Derek was curious. He could not believe that a nine-year-old girl could depose a powerful ruler quite so easily. Was it a trap of some kind? Was the old Wise Woman still dangerous? He dared not ignore anything that might endanger the rescue of Eva.

Margo clapped her hands three times, and her entire entourage rose and followed her at a discreet distance. The curtains of the litter remained closed.

"As you may have surmised from my predecessor's unfortunate physiognomy, she is in fact over a hundred years old. She was a librarian in a small town high enough in the mountains to survive the great tsunamis and tectonic earth movements that decimated the antecedent lowlands, where now stands the New Sea. Her name was Clara Johnson, and she seems to have behaved effectively both during and immediately after the cataclysm. It seems that there were vast indeterminate explosions emanating from the ancient sea floor, by the way. You've always been curious about the exact nature of the cataclysm, I believe?''

''I still am,'' said Derek. ''But right now I'd rather hear about this Clara Johnson.''

Margo nodded. ''As a young woman,'' she continued, ''Clara was evidently not without at least rudimentary intelligence, nor was she yet completely embittered by a world that failed to regard her as highly as she regarded herself. Her effectiveness during and after the cataclysm led to her being given power. And that was her undoing. I don't suppose the name Acton means anything to you? Well, he once observed that 'Power corrupts, absolute power corrupts absolutely.' Once Clara Johnson had crushed all opposition, she indulged herself in all her long suppressed desires. Rather pedestrian desires, by the bye, if her diary is any true indication.''

''Her diary?''

''I've been reading it on the way here.'' She nodded toward the litter.

Derek frowned. ''Can she be trusted? Isn't it dangerous to keep her so close to you?''

''She can be trusted to betray me at the first opportunity—cognizance of which fact may in time prove invaluable. You know that she colludes with the Brotherhood of Diablo, of course? Yes, it was rather obvious. But as to contingent periculousness, she has in fact a vested interest in my own safety and preservation. Failing my intercession, she would summarily be dismembered by her quondam subjects. In short, Clara lives only so long as I do."

Jana glanced impatiently at her; but only said, "We're almost to the beach, Margo. You still haven't told us how you became the Wise Woman."

"You recall the contests of yesterday? Well, Clara maintained the fiction of free succession to power by a similar contest in wisdom. Although her cerebral accouterments are pedestrian, they exceeded those of any challenger—until this morning. None, in fact, has challenged her in over fifty years, and absolute power was the concomitant sequela of her ostensible absolute invincibility. Her Sacred Books of Wisdom, upon which the contest was based, were merely the most imposing tomes salvaged from her small-town library. The judges were naturally her flunkies. There are still a few other people who have somehow acquired the rudiments of literacy, although, since the Wise Woman's power depended ultimately on her ability to read and interpret a few canonized texts, she had a powerful vested interest in obscuritantism. Her people were only allowed to learn a superstitious awe of her own learning—such as it is." She sniffed.

"And your knowledge of these Sacred Books of Wisdom was greater than hers?" They were now approaching the seashore hills, and he was careful to keep the procession screened from the sea. "By the way, what are they?"

"The Sacred Books of Wisdom? As I say, merely the most imposing tomes that Clara salvaged from her small-town library: *War and Peace*, *The Life of Samuel Johnson*, and *The Complete Sherlock Holmes*. I read them last night, and now I am the Wise Woman.'' Neither her paleness nor the redness about her eyelids could disguise her avidity.

Derek and Jana exchanged significant looks. They both knew Margo too well not to be apprehensive about what she might do with so much power. She was far more intelligent than the old Wise Woman, and perhaps even more cold-blooded and ruthless.

By the time Derek had made the tactical changes, the scout ship was less than a half mile off-shore; its black sails hauled down, it moved cautiously toward the beach. There were whitecaps here and there on the choppy waters, but the afternoon sky was clear, and the slanting rays of the sun made everything on shore plainly visible. Everybody on deck could see the four men despoiling the Invincible's corpse on the beach.

Peer and the three others with him made an impudent show of holding up the weapons and ornaments for inspection. There could be only one reaction from the Brotherhood of Diablo to such an outrage, and the oars of the galley once more began to beat at a rapid pace. The men despoiling the corpse did not seem to notice the ship until it was almost upon them. Only as the prow ran full tilt onto the sand did they turn and run for their lives.

Handlers and dog-things boiled over the side, followed by the grotesque, hulking forms of their masters, furious to avenge the desecration that they had just witnessed.

Then the entire beach erupted into a leaping, shouting, rock-throwing turmoil. The Brotherhood of Diablo looked upon all other peoples as mere cattle; none had ever dared resist them. But a lifetime of military drilling had conditioned their every response, and four of them, armed with swords and rectangular shields, immediately formed a screen in front of the bow. A fifth directed the relaunching of the ship. Not even the rain of missiles deterred them.

Derek himself threw the first rope; the stones twined around the mast and he pulled it taut. Two other men hammered a wooden stake firmly into the sand. Ropes flew from all sides, as Derek outflanked the wall of Invincibles and hurled himself at the side of the ship. Grabbing an oarlock, he vaulted onto the deck.

The chief slave was hacking away the grappling lines with an axe. Derek cut him down and snatched the ring of keys from around his neck.

The galley slaves were a pathetic sight: deformed, filthy, gaunt-eyed skeletons, their backs a welter of scars and festering sores. Even when Derek unlocked their chains they just sat there, too spiritless to try to escape. He actually had to drive them from their benches and over the side to get them to leave the ship. Their masters would now have to row themselves back to Diablo—if they should manage to relaunch the ship.

So far they had failed. Rows of slaves jammed their shoulders against the prow and heaved with all their might. Bellowing and cursing with rage, their master joined them with his immense weight.

The ship began to move; with so much force heaving against it, a few more minutes would surely see it back in the water. No victory over the Brotherhood of Diablo could mean anything to Derek if he lost this ship; for with it he would lose his only chance of ever rescuing Eva.

Sword in hand, he hurled himself over the rail, but before he could attack those trying to relaunch the ship, he was struck in the leg by a rock thrown by one of his own men. He staggered back into the surf. The Rathug heaving at the prow saw him—and recognized him.

"Derek the Hunter!" he screamed in rage.

That caused the whole line of those screening the ship from attack to whirl around. They recognized him too, and in their anger they forgot everything but vengeance. Though they had failed in their mission, though they now died a contemptible death at the hands of their own cattle, there was still one mighty service they could render the Brotherhood of Diablo. The first to attack Derek was a monstrosity over seven feet tall.

Derek dodged the blow, then spun aside to evade attack by the hulk who had been trying to relaunch the ship. Then he was startled by the sound of a tremendous blow; there was Gunnar, standing over the collapsed hulk, brandishing his mighty warclub.

Soon the battle was over. Once the four Rathugs defending the prow of the ship had turned their shields, they became vulnerable to the rain of missiles from the beach. Not even a lifetime of military drilling could save them from the pikes of their attackers.

It was just dusk as the last of them fell dying into the surf. The whole world seemed to erupt in joyous cheers.

Chapter 18: The Shores of Diablo

Derek wondered why so many slaves had been unable to relaunch the galley, even with the huge Rathug heaving with them. Had something snagged the hull? Repairs might take hours, and they had to reach Diablo before morning. While the preparations for departure were being hurried forward, he decided that he had better inspect the ship itself. The only thing worse than being tied up with repairs was sinking in the middle of the New Sea.

"What are you looking for?" asked Gunnar.

"I'm afraid something may have snagged the hull. Not even that big hulk you clouted was able to heave it off the beach."

Gunnar chuckled delightedly. "It was snagged all right—by me. While they were heaving at one end, I was heaving back at the other. By the way, I hear that little smartypants is now the Wise Woman. I hope she don't try any of her tricks."

"Keep an eye on her while I'm gone."

"Don't worry about that. In fact, I think she's up to something right now. What, I don't know. But she's been calling all kinds of people over to her litter for questioning, one by one."

Derek sighed. "Well, I was going to talk to her before we left anyway. It might as well be now."

Margo already knew the value of theatrics. It was dark now, and she sat regally in her litter, surrounded by a ring of torches, while her entourage hovered submissively about her like the court of an ancient potentate.

Derek bowed respectfully. He was sailing for Diablo within minutes, on the most important undertaking of his entire life, and he wanted no possible misunderstandings with the local people to delay him. Out of the corner of his eye he noticed a sneer on Clara Johnson's shrivelled old face.

Margo lifted an eyebrow, and the old woman instantly scuttled out of earshot. Then she clapped her hands three times and ordered the rest of her entourage to retire as well. They bowed and deferentially backed away.

She said in a low voice, "I have just learned that the Brotherhood of Diablo has in its possession a being with Jana's anomalous powers of perception. I have also just learned that they are even now gathering an armada against the Fisherfolk to the north, a region where, it seems, foggy weather is not uncommon. Now this being like Jana—whose uninspiring name, it turns out, is Willie—must be vital to any nautical exploit contemplated by the Rathagon. Since your actions tonight must depend largely on contingencies of which there can be no precognizance, I will only advise you also to make a concerted effort to rescue this Willie.''

Derek translated to himself: rescue Willie at all costs, and Eva if you have time. And the Fisherfolk? Was Margo already thinking of using them in some way to expand her power?

She continued, ''When you have liberated this Willie—and, of course, Eva—I would counsel you to proceed north to the realm of the Fisherfolk. Being a maritime people, they must needs have proficient shipwrights.''

''Yes, but why are you interested in shipwrights?''

''My realm abounds with ship timber at a transportable distance from the sea. Shipbuilding will profitably occupy my people while I consolidate my power.'' Derek smiled at her reference to ''my realm'' and ''my people.''

''Gunnar is a competent executor, and I shall enlist his services in the enterprise. Even a small fleet may effectively harry the armada now gathering in Colinga Harbor. By the bye, one of the self-styled Invincibles from the scout ship is still alive. He should provide useful information.''

Derek was alarmed; even one such creature on the loose could be formidable.

''The wretch is no longer dangerous,'' Margo reassured him. ''I have taken the precaution of having all his limbs fractured.''

The cold-blooded manner in which she said this alarmed Derek even more than the deed itself. But they were now signalling him from the beach: the galley was ready to sail for Diablo.

Margo smiled coldly after him as Derek ran for the ship.

The news of their victory had already reached the surrounding hills, and people were streaming in from all directions to join the celebration. The beach was now thronged; there were so many torches that Derek feared that the light might be seen all the way from Diablo.

Great quantities of food and drink were being distributed with an almost regal munificence by Margo; evidently to contrast her own reign with the niggardliness of her predecessor's. If old Clara Johnson sneered at the feasting and dancing and merrymaking, she prudently kept herself out of sight.

Getting Buck on board ship was indeed a problem. One of the dog-things released from the ship had been smart enough not to stand and fight, and Buck had chased it back and forth across the valley for miles before he finally brought it down. His head now hung from weariness, but even had he been fresh he could never have leaped over the bulwarks by himself.

Korso got some of the freed galley slaves—who had just had the first good meal of their adult lives—to rig a sling. With much heaving and cursing and growling, Buck was at last hoisted aboard. He immediately found a dark corner and curled up to sleep.

There had been three volunteers for every available place in the crew, and hundreds more swarmed over the sand to help with the relaunching. Without Gunnar heaving back at the other end, the galley slid easily into the water. Derek held Jana up so that she could see over the top of the railing. The receding beach was a carnival of torches and bonfires, and the people cheered them as if they were going forth to conquer the whole Brotherhood of Diablo.

The oars stroked the waters of the New Sea with an eagerness that they had never known before, which almost compensated for the rowers' lack of skill. Korso immediately took them in hand. He had been a galley slave for many years before becoming a handler of dog-things, and soon they were cutting the water at a goodly rate with far less effort. There was a light breeze out of the west, and they left the black sails furled.

Jana acted as navigator, keeping the ship on course for a northern promontory of Diablo. She whispered to Derek:

"That's where Willie is. I can't find Eva yet—we're still too far away—but she's certain to be nearby."

Derek hoped that this was true, but he did not want to disturb her concentration, and left her alone. She sat cross-legged at the stern of the ship. Korso was the steersman, and he watched her intently for each signal to port or starboard. He alone knew how lucky they were to have so infallible a navigator on board. The sky had grown overcast, hiding the moon and stars, and the pale phosphorescence of the New Sea cast little light.

Derek took his turn at the oars with the rest, impatient at even the steady speed that they made all through the night. Jana kept them straight on course—so long as they kept her from dozing.

"I just found Eva," she cried at last. "She's still alive, and Willie is not far away."

It was about two hours before dawn when they slipped into the rocky inlet on the northern coast of Diablo. They might have to leave again in a hurry, so Derek had the ship stand off-shore. Unloading Buck was no problem; he simply dived in and paddled for shore. Derek waded after him through the dark, chilly water with Jana on his shoulder. They reached the shore just in time to get a cold shower, as Buck shook the water out of his coat.

There was almost no beach; hulking rocks rose directly out of the surf, and they had to clamber blindly upward through the darkness. Fog drifted through the scrub forest, and the dank air chilled them to the bone.

Derek whispered, "Can you talk to Willie yet?"

She was silent for several minutes; then shook her head. "Maybe it's the fog. We're close enough, and he knows I'm here, but I can only pick up a word now and then. We'll have to get a little closer. Oh, Buck!" She shuddered as she climbed onto his back. "You're so wet!"

She pointed the way, but the rolling mist and the dense scrub forest all around them slowed their progress. Buck's huge green eyes glowed like lanterns in the dark, and Jana let him find the best paths by himself, with only a few corrective tugs at his ears. Most of the time she sat hunched to one side, as if silently listening for something.

"Derek!" she cried, sitting bolt upright. Then she was silent for a while. "Eva's all right," she said at last. "But Willie says that we're going the wrong way. There's a big ravine between us and the camp, and we have to circle inland and come up from the other side."

"Which way?"

After a long moment: "To the left. Two more ships of raiders came in during the night, and they're all drunk and gorging like beast-things." She shuddered. "They're even butchering some of the captives, and Willie has to watch it all."

"What about Eva?"

"She's chained to a post in her tent, so she can't possibly escape by herself. There's only one guard and one dog-thing on watch—mostly just to keep the drunkards away."

"What about Willie himself?"

She concentrated for a long time, then suddenly began to sob. "He says there's no way we could possibly rescue him. His cage is locked, and it's right in a corner of the biggest tent, which is packed with drunken Rathugs. They think it's funny to make him watch what they do, because he sometimes gets sick to his stomach." She wiped her eyes. "He says we should just save Eva and escape before dawn."

Bestial shouts and laughter echoed weirdly through the clammy air as they crept up on the camp from the landward side; the glow of the campfire grew brighter as they approached. Buck became harder and harder for little Jana to control.

"Just off to our right," she whispered. "There's about fifteen of them and—"

A scream of torment burst through the fog from nearby, followed by shouts of obscene, drunken laughter. Derek drew his sword and crept forward.

A fire roared greasily in the clearing among several

tents. A strange joint of meat was being turned on a spit, and hulking shapes reeled back and forth with great flagons of liquor. A naked woman hung by her wrists from the lowest bough of a tree; her feet were not quite able to touch the ground. A drunken hulk snatched something from the fire and staggered toward her. She writhed and screamed in agony, amidst a chorus of obscene laughter.

Little Jana was trembling and sobbing when Derek got back to her. This close, she was unable to ignore the minds in torment. She whispered the directions to Eva's tent and slipped away into the fog. The screaming, howling, bellowing pandemonium resounded weirdly from every direction at once. Derek never once thought of his own danger.

Buck's hackles rose and his green eyes shone in the darkness; but this was his element, and not even Derek, tiptoeing beside him, could detect the least sound of movement. The dog-thing guarding the tent certainly never did, and Derek himself dispatched the slave who had been drowsing near the entrance. He dragged the carcasses into an alley between two skin tents.

The great tent at the center of the camp was ablaze with torchlight; much of the brutish uproar came from inside. Most of the smaller tents surrounding it seemed deserted. He crept around to the front of Eva's tent and slipped inside.

A single candle guttered dimly from a pole driven into the ground; there was no bed or furnishings of any kind. Eva sat alone beside the tent's centerpost. She was awake, and their eyes met as he entered. He felt a catch in his throat as he looked down at her. She, too, felt the thrill of excitement; her eyes glittered and her high, full breasts rose and fell with her rapid breathing. Neither spoke; there was no need to say anything.

Then a scream of torment sounded from not far away, and Eva turned and began to dig into the loose earth beside her. At last she uncovered one of the metal tent spikes.

"I stole it," she whispered. "I've been trying to work this staple out of the post, but the guard keeps looking into the tent."

"He won't look any more," said Derek.

The chain ran from a metal band around her right ankle to a heavy staple driven into the centerpost; the wood around the staple was chipped and scratched. Derek moved her leg close to the staple, so that he could double the chain back on itself and use it as a fulcrum. The chipping that she had already done allowed him to get a firm bite with the tent spike, and he slowly worked the staple free, until with a last groan it fell to the earth.

She immediately wound the chain around her right leg and tied it in place. She could now run if she had to, and they crept silently to the opening.

Shadows reeled in and out of the translucent glimmer of the campfire. Then someone bellowed drunkenly, and several smaller shadows scurried obsequiously into the light; they seemed to stretch upwards into the tree, and a limp figure dropped to the ground. They picked it up and hurried away.

Derek and Eva ducked back as they passed. The slaves bore the naked body of the woman as if it was no more than a slab of meat; they carried it into the great tent at the center of the camp, where the obscene feasting was still loud. The sight made a powerful impression on both of them, a lasting impression that was to influence the course of future events. They never again spoke of merely finding some refuge from the Brotherhood of Diablo.

Buck wagged his tail at the sight of Eva, and she hugged him and roughed his ears. Jana met them just outside the camp, and she wept for joy as she greeted Eva.

"Can you still talk with Willie?" Derek whispered. "Then ask him to describe exactly where he's at, and who and what are around his cage. Please don't argue, Jana. I remember what he said. Just ask him."

While Jana stood in silent concentration, Derek drew Eva aside and explained to her all about Willie. He had kept the tent spike that he had used to free her, and now she knew how he meant to use it. She looked anxiously into his eyes for a moment, then just nodded.

Jana hurried over to them. "Willie still thinks that it's too dangerous—"

"Never mind about that. Did he tell you where he is, and how his cage is opened?"

She nodded, and repeated all that Willie had told her. Then he lifted her onto Buck's back and embraced Eva.

"Have the men standing ready at their oars," he whispered. Then he slipped silently into the fog and was gone.

They got back to the ship without incident. Eva ignored the weight of the chain on her leg as she waded through the chilly water with Jana on her shoulder. Korso had had the foresight to have the sling ready, and hoisting Buck on deck was accomplished even more smoothly than the first time. He rewarded them with a cold shower.

Then they waited. Was Derek having trouble reaching Willie's cage unseen? Had he been captured? Or killed? Jana frowned in concentration, but she was now too far away to talk with Willie. A fringe of light appeared along the eastern horizon.

"They're coming!" Jana cried suddenly. "Oh, no! Dog-things! Derek can't run very fast carrying Willie, and it looks like the whole camp is after them."

"How close are they?" asked Eva.

"About half a mile from shore, but they'll never make it." She danced up and down with apprehension. "Willie says that the dog-things are gaining."

Eva knelt beside her at the rail, with Buck at their side; he sensed that something was wrong, and stared expectantly at Jana with his huge green eyes.

"Hold out your arm," said Eva. "Point exactly to where Derek is now." Then she turned to Buck and cried, "Derek, Buck! Derek!"

He put his huge paws on the railing and dived over the side. They watched him paddle to shore, shake the water from his coat, and clamber up the boulders into the fog. Then silence.

"But Buck will never be able to find Derek in this fog, Eva," cried Jana.

"He won't have to. Just tell your little friend Willie that Buck is on the way. Let him do the finding."

"What a dummy I am sometimes," Jana muttered to herself. After a while: "They found him! They found Buck! Oh, don't be scared, Willie! That's better. Derek put him on Buck's back and . . . oh, no! They're still cut

251

off from the shore.'' She gasped. ''Don't say anything for a few minutes.''

At last she reported, ''They have to turn inland, where they'll try to hide. Derek sends a message for you. 'Sail north to the realm of the Fisherfolk. Ask them to send shipwrights to the Wise Woman. Jana will explain. You must now take command.' That's all, and . . . Oh, Eva! I can't reach him any more! They're moving away so fast!''

Eva held Jana in her arms, and tried to soothe her trembling and sobbing. Then she carried her to the stern of the ship and laid her in a comfortable nook with blankets and a pillow. The baying of dog-things could now be heard approaching the shore; the island of Diablo still lay shrouded in fog.

Eva took command, and the oars of the galley beat a steady rhythm as it glided swiftly across the rocky inlet toward the open sea. The sails were unfurled, the course set for the north. She stood at the bow, looking forward and not back.